The Distance to the End

A Novel

Michael Aaron Casares

ISBN: 978-0692667835
Published by Serasac Press
Austin, TX, United States of America

The Distance
to the End

Michael Aaron Casares

- -

When you are far away
I dream on the horizon
and words fail,
and, yes, I know
that you are with me;
you, my moon, are here with me,
my sun, you are here with me.

I'll go with you
to countries I never
saw and shared with you,
now, yes, I shall experience them.
I'll go with you
on ships across seas
which, I know
exist no longer;
with you I shall experience them again.
I'll go with you,
I with you.

~ Lucio Quarantotto

Part

~

One

1

I hit the pipe one more time. There wasn't time to wait. They'd come and then there'd be no more time. Truth is after all this time I was still into the same old thing. True the situation had changed, and definitely the scenery, but I hadn't. Not that there was anything wrong with that. You wouldn't expect a dramatic change of scenery would truly grant a dramatic change of personality, unless everything you'd previously stood for could be frivolously discarded. And truth be told, I'd played that card, too. But it wasn't important anymore.

"So, where do you want to go?"

I looked around, someone was there, a wavy blunder as I hastily scanned the room and glanced skyward. The bastard'd snuck up on me before I could exhale; I had to hold the itching smoke inside. The pipe was in my hand. He hadn't noticed. I blew it in his face. He stepped back and coughed.

"What the hell are you doing out here?"

I had been interrupted. "I'm getting ready." I turned and looked to him. It was funny. "I haven't decided yet." I walked to the mirror, the bureau it sat on glinted. "There is only one point to this anyway."

"So, then we might as well get to it."

The sun was high in the distance as we rode out onto the

terrain. A long time ago Raoul and I had been out on the road. Some chick told us she could picture us traveling throughout the countryside on motorcycles. So I went out and got a motorcycle. I didn't know if he would fancy traveling on a bike and for a time I entertained the idea of getting Raoul the sidecar that attached, but opted to just let him get his own bike. We both had non-descript rice-burners. They rode smoothly and purred steadily as the ground raced beneath us. I never cared for Harley's, or hog-like motorcycles. They seemed too bulky and cumbersome. I saw nothing aesthetic about them. The weather was temperate and provided for easy riding. We were moving fast to the west. We were going to do it right if we were going to do it this way and there was no better way to do it. I'm a fourth generation American, and I felt it necessary to establish a certain aspect of my character. I had once traced my family's history and near as I could tell on both sides my family went back at least three generations in the country. Not long as some, but longer than most talking heads on corporate television. But that wasn't what I was here to do. I wasn't here to talk politics. I was here for only one reason.

We'd ridden all day through some unknown terrain, through the barren desert plains of the American West: rolling hills and mountains, flatlands and dry brush, the constant signs warning against hagglers and escaped convicts. How we even managed such a feat was beyond me. My head swam as the sun began to set. It seemed the moon was on the other side creeping up slowly. What was the memory locked on the inside? It was warmly fuzzy. There was a point to this, but I couldn't remember. I looked up. I looked skyward. I tried to remember. The bike purred beneath me. I hugged it tightly against my body. Suddenly, there was a horn and confusion and fear. We had meant to do it right. If this was what we were gonna do. We were gonna drive into town on a cool March day and have at it unlike any had heard before. We'd try and show up Shakespeare, but there was no guarantee of that. Especially considering the point. We were nothing like Shakespeare after all. We were more on par with an open mic session at the local coffee bar. We were more like a cheap, two-bit circus that takes place once a month, praising literacy and struggling behind petty, bureaucratic styling. Everything blurred. I didn't even know where Raoul was anymore.

The taste of dirt in my mouth was grainy and coarse. I couldn't see anything. Dust clouds swelled. My left leg felt heavy. It was pinned beneath the bike. I still felt its warm purr as I hugged the bike tight. I heard more horns and sirens and a stifling of wind.

There was no use to it. I lift my head up. The dirt was gone. The dust clouds were gone. The road and bike were gone. The sky was gone. Everything was gone and replaced by a somber blue that was cast upon everything, and the shadows and the comfort of my blankets were all I felt, and the warm purring was Raoul who lay beside me, cuddling as we warmed each other. Raoul had noticed I'd awakened. He lifted his head.

"What's the matter?"

"I started with a dream." I paused still half asleep, "Now I've gone and tricked them."

Raoul seemed to understand what I was talking about. He responded, "Well, that's a bit rude, now isn't it?"

"Yeah, I guess, so."

"Just go to bed. When you wake up in the morning you can worry about it."

"K."

We fell asleep.

2

When I woke Raoul was gone. The sun shined in from the window. Raoul had pulled back the curtains and opened the shade, his way of gently waking me. It was my favorite way to wake alone. Birds twittered outside. I could see a deep blue beyond the blinds. No clouds.

"Wakey! Wakey!" his voice came from the other side of the room, but he was soon on top of me, the full weight of his body on me, his legs straddling me and locking me under the blankets. I couldn't move. "Get up, it's a beautiful day!" He kissed my cheek, the stubble of his chin tickling my skin. Then he rolled off me and disappeared out of the room. I rolled out of bed, the blankets still wrapped around me. I put my slippers on. The room was bright, everything white against thin hardwood floors and a matched bedroom set. I went to the bathroom, washed up and headed downstairs. Breakfast was cooking.

"I went to the market this morning." Raoul commented as I entered the room. "Sleep okay?" His back was to me as he busied over the stove, cooking bacon and eggs. I slept wonderfully, all but the dream. It wasn't unnerving or anything, but it did stick out.

"Yeah, I did. You're up early." We were new to the neighborhood, hadn't been there more than a month. I had never been anywhere new in my life. That's not to say, I hadn't traveled much, I just never moved before.

"I know. I kinda wanted to see how the neighborhood is, you know, go for a nice morning walk, all that good stuff. Very fresh day out. Kinda makes me want a dog or something." He shot me a glance out of his eyes, his way of testing the waters. I got off the stool and walked over to him. He was so adorable. I brushed his black hair from his forehead and kissed his temple and hugged him, he leaned into me a little.

"Maybe we'll get a dog." Raoul smiled up and kissed me, I kissed him back and he returned to the eggs, flipping the sunny side over.

"Anything you need to do today?" I asked.

"No, I just need to finish getting ready if we're leaving for the weekend."

I had forgotten. I wasn't even mentally ready for what was to come.

"Did you forget?" Raoul laughed lightly.

"No, not at all." I lied. But it was okay.

"Yeah. Gladys and Neville will be here soon so we should probably hustle."

We hadn't seen Gladys and Neville since we moved to our new place. It was nice to have them over. It would be nice to have anyone over. None of our friends had seen our new place. Not that we were trying to be secretive, but we had been busy, among other things. Gladys and Neville had been longtime friends of both of us, though I had known Neville since high school, so he and I had been acquainted the longest. Neville met Gladys during college. She was the instructor's niece. The instructor was also a coke dealer, so consequently she was the coke dealer's niece. Neville, never one to shy away from anything that caught his eye, wooed his way into the heart of the coke dealer's niece. I personally always thought the universe had a unique way of connecting us conveniently with everything we needed when we needed, and I'll leave it at that.

The two had been clean of drugs since they'd been married,

[13]

though Gladys always remarked to me her desire to try some. One incident found me in a bathroom with her at a concert where she suddenly whipped out a glass pipe and begged me to get high with her. I'd never done crack before, and hadn't wanted to. Fortunately for me she took the majority of the tiny rock she'd burned. I tasted the faint metallic numbing on my lips, the back of my throat, a brief seizing in my lungs and exhaled. My eyes bubbled. Someone knocked on the door, like a pounding.

"Whoa, occupied!" Gladys yelled.

She had told me she really didn't do these things anymore, but she just came across it and felt better doing it with someone. She asked me not to tell Neville, just because she had promised him she wouldn't blaze out anymore, because they really had calmed that part of their life. I felt kind of guilty playing her accomplice, but I told her I wouldn't say a thing. Then a pounding at the door resounded again. I thought maybe it was the bass from the music.

"Hold up!" She yelled, the pipe already put away. She opened the door.

"Where do you think we'll stay?" Raoul asked, zapping me back to reality.

"Oh, I don't know. It doesn't really matter, anywhere'll be fine. If I know Nev, he'll wanna stay some place bangin'."

"Cool."

The last few months had been very nice. They had been quiet, life slowing to a day-by-day pace. It had been a while since I hung out with friends and just relaxed.

Raoul and I finished breakfast chatting like honeymooners, all thanks to Raoul, whose lightened disposition made for pleasant company. Then we packed for the week long journey as music filled the house from our 1970's turntable, digital rhythms and electronic beats dancing through the halls.

3

A knock came at the door. I had heard Gladys and Neville pull up. They didn't call. That was Neville's style. Of course, I'd told him that was rude, but he never seemed to mind. Gladys kinda' just went along with what he did. They were both rebels in their own right. Neville was headstrong about his views and about following through with ideas he fashioned, no matter what the idea. Gladys had been a drug user, undoubtedly as the niece of a narcotics dealer, and had a history to go with the lifestyle (a history I feared someday she'd try to remedy, and it was how she may try to remedy it that scared me). Still these were good friends of mine, they'd been married for a couple of years, and they seemed well beyond the honeymoon stage.

I opened the door. There stood Gladys and Neville in all their glory: Gladys in neon pink leopard skin boots and matching shawl, and Neville in brown, brushed felt pants.

"Hey, buddy, what's up?" shouted Neville. Gladys smiled.

"Hi Nick, how are you?" I hugged them as they entered.

"Nice house you got here, buddy, looks like you found a good spot."

"Yeah, it has a lot of curb appeal. I can't wait to see the rest of it." Gladys commented.

I walked them through the foyer, into the living room. The house was really modest, and not all that new or big, but good enough for two. The living room opened up into the kitchen, with a bar and island. It made for a spacious room. Raoul was in the kitchen getting glasses.

"Hi, guys!" Raoul greeted.

"Raoul!" Gladys exhaled and walked immediately over, her arms in the air, raring for a hug.

Raoul met her half way, "How are you doing, Gladys? You look great." They embraced.

"Thank you, Raoul. It's so nice to see you again! It's been so long."

"You're telling me. I was wondering what ya'll been up to."

"Well you could have called." Gladys laughed. Neville and I had already made our way to the kitchen. Raoul and Gladys followed.

"How's it going, Raoul?" Neville said shaking Raoul's hand and slamming a heavy hand on his back. Raoul flinched slightly.

"Good, how've you been?"

"Great, doing great." Neville glanced around. "So what we got going on here? What's to drink?"

"Oh," said Raoul, "Whatever. We have some juice, some pop. Purified water."

"Purified." Neville chuckled, "What's the difference, a few chemicals? Ha!" Neville knew our thoughts on drinking supply. Needless to say, we didn't cook with tap water, let alone drink it. Still, Neville always liked to egg things on.

"How about a beer?" Neville suggested.

"Gonna start the party early, huh?" I smiled at Neville.

"Well, if we're gonna do it, we may as well do it right." Neville started in and produced a case of beer from the leather jacket he had folded over his arm. It was his favorite brand, Basura Blanco, a five-pack case that came with five shots of tequila. Neville had served up shots and passed around the beers in no time.

"You guys are crazy." Gladys commented, pulling a four-pack of chardonnay from her purse. The tiny plastic bottles perspired, comfortably chilled. She passed on the shots, preferring wine instead. Neville seemed to have absolutely no problem with this. Then we gave them the customary home tour, beer in hand.

We took them through the space, reaching the master bed room. The color and windows opened up the room, making it bigger than it seemed. There was a seat on the bay window, the closets hid behind sleek walls, even some of the shelving was built into the walls. The only objects protruding were a mirrored chest, the bed and side tables. We walked to the en suite. Neville looked in, exclaimed, and turned to look at the bedroom again. Gladys walked in, grabbing my hand behind me.

"Oh, my god, this is so nice!" she said, fumbling with something in her hands. "And I love the color." She laughed. She turned around quickly and in a single motion held a fingernail up to my nose. She sniffed emphatically. I mimicked her sniff, inhaling deeply and casually, so as to remain inconspicuous. Gladys smiled, turned around, reloaded and inhaled the fine white powder. She wiped her nose and walked out. The back of my nose felt full and stuffed as the junk slowly moved back and down my throat like a dry lump of snot. I felt my heart palpitate, my body bracing for that long-ago, familiar rush. My pupils narrowed and expanded. I drank some beer.

"So, who's driving?" I asked stepping into the middle of everyone.

"Driving? Who said anything about driving? We can't drink and drive!" Neville took a swig of his beer, "We're flying, man."

"Flying? You've got to be insane. It's only a few hours' time."

"Yeah, well, we'll cut it down to a few minutes, whatta ya' say?" Neville put his arm around my shoulder.

"But we haven't got tickets. What time do we depart? We have to get through security and all that, you know."

Neville through his head back and laughed facetiously. "Who needs to bother with that?"

I looked at him a bit apprehensively, "You got a plane, or what?" I asked.

Neville burped, "Yeah, I have a plane. And a pilot."

*   *   *

Neville had always told me that from a very young age he pictured himself as the type of individual who was very successful and powerful. He dreamed big. He said at the age of five instead of playing Ninja Turtles with his friends, he was the commander of a vast army, busting down the doors of citizens and exerting his force. Fortunately, Neville had no military experience, and probably never would. There were other things about his aspirations that were more humble, opening a business or something that would generate net worth or fame, or both. What he hadn't told me, as he explained on the way to a private airfield, was that he had won the lottery. I was stoked for him, and could certainly understand why they had insisted on paying for the trip. A private airplane was something he always wanted, and flying from western California to Las Vegas was a quick trip by plane. Neville was ebullient. We could drink, we could just relax. Neville also knew, as well as Raoul and Gladys, that to fly, this would be my preference: private and not having to deal with the hoopla of current airport security. Gladys had also had a recent, unpleasant run-in with airport security, and for all the joys of recreational drug-use, was understandably happy with the private plane.

We landed smoothly, buzzed off a bottle of champagne Neville had been saving for his plane's maiden voyage. He was tempted to smash it along the side the vessel, but we had convinced him to drink it instead. Flying into Las Vegas was fun. At first there was nothing but deserts and mountains, a view of Hoover Dam in the distance, and then a run of homes and retail centers leading to the strip of new hotels and casinos, all tiny little boxes growing, growing, until the magnificence of the strip became bigger than us. The grandeur and verbosity of the city often overplayed in the movies and on television, you had to get onto the boulevard itself before you truly felt its magic. My heart smiled as the wheels touched down and we bounced ever so slightly in Neville's nondescript personal plane, and the personal pilot, like personal pilots in the imaginations of all, cleared us to exit, opened the hatch, and dropped the stairs. Neville stood at the top, a wily prince with an empty glass once full of champagne.

"Now that's how I arrive!" he screamed, and threw down his glass, it shattering on the concrete. He stepped down; we all followed. The pilot opened a hatch on the back and began to unload our luggage. There was a short stretch limo idling nearby. Raoul smiled. The sky was blue and the sun was bright, a stiff breeze carried the heat away and cooled the tarmac.

4

The stretch limo was what I would have expected in a place like Las Vegas. I had only ridden in a limo once before, for my sister's wedding when I was a kid. This was nothing like it: party lights lined the ceiling, neon and fiber optic lights accented the walls beneath the windows and lined the floor as well, there was a mini bar and several glasses and mugs, two mini flatscreen televisions were in the corner near the driver's side which, naturally, had a privacy window tinted black. I wondered if Neville had bought the limo, too, but he had only rented. It took us to our hotel.

Las Vegas Boulevard was "the Strip," the main drag for some time now. The original hot spot of Casino Center in downtown Las Vegas was now roofed by a Technicolor ceiling hosting millions of LED-lights and a mega amped sound system a few blocks long. It was a dream wonder to drunks and druggies walking the streets to live up the Sin City reveries of revelry and excess. I couldn't wait to go. I was grateful to be included on this trip, grateful to have Raoul by my side.

Neville told us all about his winnings. He had lucked out on a scratch off, buying it on a whim. As he recounted, he was in the local grocer and he happened to walk by the lottery ticket machine. It was a new hi-tech digital one with a bunch of flashing lights and buttons. You know, the type to attract the kiddies. He hadn't thought about playing. He only had twenty dollars, but something stopped him dead in his steps. "*Neville.*" It called him (yes, he said the machine literally called him), "*Neville, come and play.*" Neville's instinct said, play the weekly grand ticket, "Check's in the Mail." It only cost two dollars. But, no, this calling was much stronger, it said, "*Spend big, win big.*" He knew he'd have to play more. The twenty popped into the machine for "Triple Your Treasure." Scratch off and reveal your winning number to win the prize printed below. His winning numbers were five, nine, twenty-four, twenty-one, eighteen, and thirty-three. He scratched the five rows frantically, taking no time for ceremony. Half way down the middle column, almost dead smack center, the number thirty-three appeared. The number beneath it, and the amount of zeroes that followed it, made Neville's heart drop. He held in his hands a ticket worth a million dollars. He couldn't believe it. He was in the middle of the store and didn't know how to react. His knees were weak. He needed to sit down. Should he jump for joy? No. He didn't want to call attention to himself. He pulled his wallet out, stuck the ticket in the billfold and put it in his front pocket. He ran out of the store.

Neville had forgotten about his plans for the day. He was supposed to pick up Gladys when she got out of work. She had gone in early that day so she would be out early. Then they were going to go pay some bills and maybe pick up a quick dinner. He got in his car and headed downtown to the official Lottery Office. He had seen it several times. He never imagined he might actually win it, never thought someday he would be on his way to a big jackpot. He knew he wouldn't be able to cash the ticket at the grocery store. No, they couldn't handle that type of money. He would have to go to the boss for this one. He smiled inside.

It was outside the official Lottery Office that Neville had realized something. He had forgotten to scratch off the "Triple Your Win" game: reveal three treasure chests to instantly triple your win! He paused before going in. His heart sank. A million dollars was great, but three million? Now here was a gamble. Neville decided he wasn't going to scratch the treasure chests. He would go in unscratched and see what kind of luck he really had.

A portly woman sat there, pale skin with red hair cotton balled in a round mound above her head. He hadn't even said hello, he just walked straight up to her and handed her the ticket. She took the ticket, scanned it and punched the serial number into her computer. Her eyes lit up.

"Good heavens!" She exclaimed, "You've hit the jackpot. Congratulations, sir!" She shuffled through paper work, her fingers fidgeting. "Just a moment, sir," she said, eyeing Neville seductively, "I just have to make a phone call." She reached for the phone. "Hello, sir. Yes, sir. I have a claim here I'll need you to authorize." She paused and looked at Neville, "Three million, sir." Neville's heart sank. "Yes, sir. Triple Your Treasure. A scratch off game, sir." She looked at Neville again and pursed her lips, her eyes narrowed, "I know, sir. I thought so, too." The woman closed the phone, congratulated Neville again, and instructed him to fill out some paper work, after which she explained all the legalese and tax information he needed to know, and wrote up a big check placard and took some pictures. Neville was expressly clear with her that he didn't want to have his name and picture advertised and all over the news. There was no way he was going to put up with long lost cousins popping up out of nowhere or anything, because he was sure he had a lot of them.

Neville told me he appreciated me for all I had done for him, which, to be honest, I didn't recall being much, but I was his best man at his wedding, so I must have done something right by him. He had planned this trip because he'd always wanted to go to Vegas, especially because I raved about it every time I went. He thought this the perfect extension of gratitude; the reciprocity of which was great.

"Hey, guys, have you another shot!" I'd been buzzing since

we made it to the airfield. We had continued our celebration in the air, drinking champagne and taking shots, and had continued in the limo, taking shots and drinking beer. My gut began to bulge a little. Raoul sat next to me, smiling and laughing, looking out the window and sipping his beer. He'd never been to Vegas before. Las Vegas Boulevard flashed before his eyes: the hotels, the people, the restaurants and shops streaming by; the architecture, a mix of new and old décor, modern and stylized creating a different world, and truly a different world from life off the strip; a swath of colored lights from modest to baroque, neo-classic to hi-tech chiming like Christmas lights even in the daylight; the signs were huge and animated advertising shows and restaurants and nightclubs, all in shimmering LED and arrant neon and trimmed with Palm Trees and Astroturf. The people, taking pictures, all with drinks and shopping bags in hand, some classy looking, others obviously obliviously touristy, others locals, a few bums here and there. This was certainly a playground for the adults. A truck whizzed by with women on all fours, their breasts hanging and robust, and their eyes commanding you to attention, the fiery background in front of which they posed red and burning. "Call now for a hot, fun time: Sin City Babes." Raoul laughed. My head was beginning to spin.

"Man, this is crazy, man! I can't believe I'm back in Vegas." I relished and then asked, "What do you want to do first?"

"Chill first, dude! I wanna check out the hotel and see what's going on there." Neville said.

"You haven't even told us where we're going. Which one is it?" Raoul said.

"All I'm gonna say is we're gonna party with the stars!" Neville's phone rang, he answered it, only slightly drunk: "Talk to me!"

The grandeur of new construction. The new Las Vegas for a new millennium as many Vegas legends either bit the dust or were remade to fit the newer, vogue and aesthetic—which in most cases was modern and sleek, or beyond baroque. While classics like CircusCircus, The Flamingo, The Riviera, The Tropicana, and all the old spots in Casino Center downtown, reminded us of times that were—the new construction literally made the place feel like an adult Disney World.

Gladys reached into her purse, fumbling through her personals.

"Hey, guys, I almost forgot! We gotta break in the limo!" I knew what that meant instantly. My heart smiled. "There's no sense making Vegas wait!" Gladys pulled a joint from a tin. It was fat and even.

"Let me see that!" I said and snatched it from her hand (improper smoking etiquette and rude I might add, but I was drunk already). I could tell by looking at it she had used a rolling machine. One couldn't roll so perfectly and evenly smooth a joint from your typical ZigZag unless cutting or double wrapping, and we all know how amateur a double wrap looked. Still, I admired the craftsmanship. I smelled it. It was spicy. It was definitely not run-of-the-mill *ganja*. No, this was at the least, a medium grade hydroponic. There was only one way to be sure.

"Here ya' go." I handed the joint back to Gladys, who was actually smiling goofily. "Smells great!"

"I know this is great; it's some good stuff, let me tell you! I got it just for the trip!" Gladys lit the joint, the first puff briefly masking her face. She inhaled again and passed to Neville, who rejected (he always rejected).

"C'mon, Neville, it's Vegas, baby, you gotta' take a hit at least off this j. It's the first j of the trip!"

Neville waved his hand in the air, as if to shoo Gladys off, then he motioned to hand him the joint. Gladys smiled gleefully and complied. Neville took a quick hit and passed to me. I offered Raoul the hit to be a gentleman.

"No, go ahead, Nicky." Raoul always knew my favorite. My

love affair with Maryjane had been a long one. I hit the joint. Surely the spice tingled in my throat, but I hadn't expected the reaction. My lungs flamed and itched. I immediately began to cough, and cough, and cough. Raoul laughed, as did Gladys. I handed him the joint. The rotation continued.

Traffic was busy, but not overwhelming. Soon, our limo slowed and turned.

"Alrighty, guys, our rooms are ready." Neville sat up, meaning to put his hand on his knee, but he misjudged and fell forward, screaming as he went down. "Oh shit!" He laughed, "Dammit, I get dizzy when I smoke!" We all started laughing. "Shut up!" He yelled, which only made us laugh harder.

"Now, as I was saying," Neville spoke after we'd composed and he'd straightened up proper. "Our rooms are ready. I think you'll enjoy them very much." He said all with a manner of pride in his eyes for now Neville was doing what he always said he'd do, he was being what he always said he'd be, a badass. And in Las Vegas, in his own right, he deserved to be treated like one.

"Badass." I said.

Neville smiled and nodded. We pulled into our hotel.

5

In this the 2000th era of current history, and to whom ever it is or was who decided how said history was crafted and recorded, there was an ever expansive awakening, the topic of which is neither here nor there, nor does it have a place in this story, but suffice it to say, the awakening was one of moral uprightness and a rejuvenated sense of empathy for fellow man. Of course, you wouldn't get the sense of this from watching cable media news or anything mainstream organized. Newspapers and popular blogs included. These outlets of negativity and fear pornography recognized long-ago this was the content that sold and created loyal patrons. There were still places, however, where one could give in to the supposed debauchery that ruins the soul. This grand awakening (the enlightening which perhaps I could discuss at a later time) would show such decisions were in fact merely the preferences of the experiencer and not something so condemning. The city to which we found ourselves was such a place, a clichéd notion of the American mythos. As the landscape had changed, however, so too had the mythology. But the newer, suave Vegas still provided all the amenities any traveler may be inclined to partake in while away in that clichéd city of the West. There were all types of entertainment: buffets that easily appeased the heftiest glutton, copious amounts of liquor so ubiquitous the image of a martini or foot-long margarita came to mind at the thought of Las

Vegas, there was sex and drugs breathing hot on the necks of all who walked about.

Neville cracked a beer open. We stood at the expansive panoramic window in Neville and Gladys' suite at the Planet Hollywood Hotel and Casino; it overlooked the Paris Hotel and the Bellagio fountains. The spectacle of the strip caused my mouth to froth.

"To lady luck!" Neville hoisted his beer up high and knocked it back.

"Ooh, you should wait to cheer lady luck until you hit the casino," I jibed.

"I may as well get as many brownie points as I can."

"Neville, you're not gonna gamble away your fortune, are you?" Gladys interjected.

"You're not gonna snort it away are ya?" Neville said looking out the window.

"What?!" She tossed a chic black leather pillow at him.

"I said I only brought a few thou, babe!" We all laughed. "After all, I gotta open my business."

"To free enterprise!" I said, cracking another beer.

"No politics! No, Nick! We're in freakin' Vegas, baby! There's a freakin' Jacuzzi in the living room and we're surrounded by Bruce Willis shit! That's fuckin' awesome!"

As a child in Mexico, Neville grew up on a healthy diet of Bruce Willis and Silvester Stallone flicks, though Neville hastens to admit he acquired his warlike nature before exposure to the likes of Rambo.

"Well, then here's to your business!" I hoisted my beer.

"Here, here!" Neville cracked his beer and chugged down half the content before spitting up projectile hops and coughing and whooping like a maniac. We could always depend on Neville to be the first to make the mess, but that is what this alpha male did, he claimed his territory, and the Bruce Willis suite was definitely his. It fitted him and Gladys. They were both diehard. Raoul and I had the Marilyn Monroe suite.

"Are you gonna gamble, too, Nicky?" Raoul asked.

"Just a little, babe."

"Holy shit!" Gladys exclaimed from another room. It was the kitchen. "This mother is loaded with alcohol. Bottles!"

"Ooh! I want a Cosmo!" Raoul popped up and ran to Gladys.

"Jack Honey rocks, babe," I called, and turned to Neville. He stood nose to windowpane, taking in the sight. "So what's the plan, man? Whatchoo wanna do?"

"Hell." I sincerely don't think he knew what to do.

"You wanna check the strip, get a bite to eat, catch a show... shit, there's a hell of a lot of things we could do."

"I never imagined I'd be here, man." Neville said dreamily, staring at the people marching up and down the strip.

"You've arrived."

"Yes, and we're gonna do this the right way!" He turned to me, his eyes wide, "What happens in Vegas—"

"Please, this story is clichéd enough," I interjected, in hopes of saving what little was left for the reader to disparage. "What is it you are planning to do in Vegas? Prostitution? High stakes gambling?" I asked him, "Are you gonna put your plane up for wager?"

"Jesus, man, I'm with Gladys." He was suddenly serious, even with the slight slurring of words, "And I plan to hold onto as much of that money as I can for as long as I can. I don't wanna be known as the 'throw away lottery winner,' you know, 'a two-year-millionaire.'"

"I got a Cosmo!" Raoul waltzed back in the room, nearly on tip toe with a martini glass in one hand and a cocktail glass in the other. He sniffed deeply a few times and came over to me. "One, Jack Honey on the rocks," He handed me the drink and kissed me

[28]

on the cheek. He wiped his nose and sniffed again. I might have guessed what he and Gladys were up to in the kitchen.

"Thank you." I said as Raoul sat. Gladys came into the room with some sort of concoction in a Brewtus mug. It looked fruity.

"Awesome drinks! Neville! Go get something!"

"You didn't get me a drink?"

"Was I supposed to? I thought you had a beer."

"I got Nick a Jack and Honey on the rocks." Raoul was bopping his head and tapping on the seat to some unheard music. He said, "We should get a radio in here."

"Well, I'm just wondering what you guys want to do."

"*Calmate, guey*, we have all day long."

"I want to check out the strip," Gladys said.

"Me, too!" Raoul seconded.

"I'm cool with that." I said.

"What about my drink?" Neville inquired.

6

Gladys bumped me up again before we headed out to the Strip. In fact, she bumped me up pretty good, a few keys worth, and I needed it because I was already so drunk and high I was wavy with a little bit of yawn. Hey, much had been accomplished in a single midafternoon that included a lot of boozing.

We walked around the PH a bit, my ears ringing with the bells and alarms of the slots and games. It was a token symphony in Vegas, the sounds of the casino. This hotel casino, dimly lit with silent neon, had modern and quasi-futuristic architecture and lacked the cigarette haze most casinos accustomed. The place was hip, the ceilings high up. Escalators led to nightclub entrances and viewing balconies lined with lemon-yellow neon ribbons that faded to electric blue to magenta to indigo, purple and green. High wire lamps hung from up top and shadowed lower planks of light that brightened players' view ever so slightly. For all the lights and twinkling, the casino still seemed dimly lit. All sorts of slot machines filled the perimeter of the joint with the poker and craps tables, the roulette and blackjack tables central.

My heart nearly stopped when, in the middle of the casino, a song began to play. It rose gradually over the melee of casino noises and suddenly, from the very shadows of the casino itself, a crowd of people appeared and started dancing, dancing to the song as if on cue. The group seemed to be led by a cute guy in a black

suit and a chubby bearded man, also in a black suit, who donned a
backwards white baseball cap. Both men were brandishing their cell
phones and digital recorders as they moved. Then there were
people everywhere doing the same. I had suddenly become the
unsuspecting drunk, and had I not been intoxicated in a mixture of
choice venoms I may have realized what was happening was a flash
mob, not uncommon in this day, but alarming to the unprepared.

As I looked around at the orgy of people, some whom were
decked out in club attire and other stand-out and modest garments,
everyone's arms in the air, people spinning in circles, one fellow
break dancing, popping up and down effortlessly, I saw Gladys and
Raoul dancing and jumping around and Neville just above them
standing on slot machine chairs pumping his fists and raising the
roof. I briefly wondered if they were in on it and suspected not as
an attendant began waving at Neville to get off the chair. I laughed
and spun around and began dancing, too, and swaying my arms and
twisting and dipping and the scene felt so unrealistic, people
everywhere holding up their phones, recording, transmitting the
sudden eruption. Crowds formed around the mob, some puzzled,
some thrilled. Security gathered. I moved and jumped, watched the
others revel the same, the music pumped and spiked the ears, and
then it was over just as it started and everyone cheered and I
cheered and Raoul ran over to me and threw his arm around my
shoulder and he was laughing and jumping up and down and I was
laughing and I was wired and my heart was racing.

"Come on guys, let's go hit the Strip!" Neville called, still on
the chairs. He was wide eyed and laughing maniacally.

"Sir, you are going to have to come down from those chairs,
sir. Sir, do you know how dangerous this is?" A game attendant
scolded Neville.

"Oh, well, give me a hand." Neville said, reaching for the
attendant.

"Nevy! C'mon, let's go!" Gladys called. She ran to him, he

stumbled clumsily to the floor and balanced himself. The four of us laughed and headed out of the casino into the bright, sunny afternoon.

*　　*　　*

Gladys and Neville walked ahead of Raoul and me. Neville and Gladys had argued a bit over whether to take a limo or not, but Gladys insisted we walked, which I agreed with because I thought we would see more of the sites if we walked. Being that it was Raoul's first time in Vegas, I insisted. Neville surrendered to Gladys' will. Three of us slurped on foot-long margaritas we'd purchased in the shops in the Miracle Mile. It was relieving to note through the cubicling, materialistic sprawl of corporatedom there was still escape into cavernous intoxication. Otherwise, how could one stand it? The same corporate, materialist, wealth design and motive everywhere you look. It all melted into the same blob when I was spent and tired. I had done this a few times before. I knew what I faced when I approached this venture and indeed, for some reason I enjoyed it. Give me a foot-long margarita any day and I would be fine, believe you me.

The sun was bright, but the weather fair. We walked south on the strip toward MGM, with the Excalibur castle and the faux Statue of Liberty towering across the street.

We took the crossing bridge at MGM to get to the other side of the boulevard, heading towards the Cosmopolitan. Gladys had a fit at Dior and Gucci, and Chanel and Versace. She hit the big names, the mainstays of the nouveau riche. Between curtains of crystals and ringing slot machines, pausing momentarily to slip a twenty into its mechanical apparatus, winning double, triple, losing and in the end quadrupling. *Double Diamond, Triple Diamond, Blazing 8's, Lucky 7's.* I manned the electronic roulette table and it never played so good, and I really wasn't a roulette kind of person. Still

[32]

the crowds, a mix of all races, a mix of all classes, some casual, some formal, some somewhere in between, kept cheering us on, and the cocktail waitress kept bringing us martinis. It was a great time. The accolades, the bells and whistles, the gambling crowds began to get to me. I felt a blackness come on. Gladys must have seen me because the next thing I knew she was by my side holding my margarita.

"Hey, buddy, what's up? You doin' okay?" She giggled and I nodded, "What say we go get some fresh air real quick?" Gladys turned. Raoul and Neville were still paying attention to the game. "Hey, guys, we're gonna get some air. Hold our numbers down, would ya?"

We walked away from the maddening crowd toward the bathroom. I wobbled ever so slightly. The booze from daylong drinking sloshed around in my brain.

"You sure you okay?" Gladys asked.

"Yeah, fine, just you know, I think everything is catching up to me is all." I turned and gave her a grin and raised my eyebrows emphatically. "We did just up and fly over here drinking all the way, you know. Good lord, what have I mixed so far?" I tried to recount my drinks.

"Come on, let's go to the bathroom." She pulled me towards the restroom. The Cosmo was considered a high end casino and resort. The décor of crystals and walls of glass, the modern and posh fixtures, not many penny slots—the place reeked of big money and was designed to attract the young and hip.

As we headed toward the bathrooms, Gladys gave me my margarita back, but discreetly slipped something else into my hand. It was a teeny-tiny, little baggy. It was stuffed with white powder. I didn't look at it long. I knew what it was immediately. Gladys smiled.

"Go ahead," she said, "That should keep you on your toes." Gladys walked into the women's restroom without looking back. I didn't know what to think. Gladys had bestowed upon me a nice wealth of "snow." A bump never hurt anybody. My palms moistened. I walked into the bathroom, the room low lit and adorned in modern, tempered neon. I opened the stall door, my heart already palpitating, a grin cracking the corners of my mouth. I was horrified by my body's natural reaction to the drug, but could care less at that point. At that point, it was all about securing the door and carefully inserting my key into the fine powder. But a baggy such as this, full as it was, could prove to be a problem. I didn't want to spill anything. Neville had done something like that once when we were in college. He dropped damn near the entire twenty on the elevator floor and we held the "door close" button down as long as we had to until we could sop up the coke with our wet palms and lick it up, dirt, dust and floor particles all. That was a helluva day, and I wasn't about to do that in the men's room of an upscale Vegas hotel. No, my anticipation gave way to deliberate, graceful engagement. The key, the longest on the ring, mounted by a dune of fine white powder glided effortlessly through the air to the recess of my nostril and lift into my nasal passage where it did what it did best (which for reality's sake we won't get into). I bumped the other nostril to keep them even, flushed the toilet, took one final large sniff and walked out feeling buzzed and waking up. I swallowed the lump dripping down my throat. It was thick and felt like it was blocking the passage. I gulped several times. Sniffed again. Outside the bathroom, Gladys was waiting, wiping and sniffing her nose.

7

Things weren't always peaches and cream for Raoul and me. We had gone through a rough patch before; we had even split for a while. It was the most pensive, consternation-absorbed fit of a time in my experience. It was necessary, but a damn bugger to work it out. Seven years was a long time. Raoul had changed in those seven years. I don't know how or why, but for some reason, I knew he wasn't quite the same.

We were young lovers to start, having courted one another for long enough a time, eventually embracing what seemed inevitable. We were idealistic and naïve back then, believing we could take the world on by ourselves, secluding ourselves in our little bubble of love. We merged, and it was nice until life became all parties and boozing. Then it became too much for Raoul. It was a pain, and marijuana was a pain because he couldn't get high on it, but when I smoked I became a vegetarian zombie, and I did it so much he began to loathe the herb. Cocaine was where he drew the line. That was it for him. He did not wish to see me fall into the depths of usage and whatever lifestyle he imagined it would create. So we parted ways for seven years, which wasn't long considering the vastness of time itself, but long enough. And seven years later we were back on again. Raoul seemed to like the party now, he even seemed to like cocaine and showed me ways of using I had never thought or tried before. Raoul teaching me was new for me, but I figured, *what the hey*. I kind of liked it, he being more dominant over I, the student, and he seemed to get off on the reversed roles as well.

Still, it plagued me at times, the uncertainty. Uncertainty was only what could be expected. A first break in a relationship and reconciliation is still a first break, and may make a second break easier. Oh, the paranoid lover's logic. This time around I did not want to be the paranoid lover. I was going to be cool about everything, though firm in my resolve. Where in this world there are men and women who jump from lover to lover, temporary spouses in this dog-use-dog world, I was in the class of people who decided to try finding myself before moving on. I had to find something in that inherently mechanized process of becoming.

Nothing had caused me to think Raoul was up to no good. I didn't allow any remnants of the past to cinder in the recesses of my imagination, though from time to time I felt the tickle at the base of my skull, a waver in my chest as if hollowing. I knew the feeling all too well. One thing I'd developed towards the end of that first time with Raoul was to trust my "gut feeling." Have you ever heard of the gut feeling? The sixth sense, intuition, first-thought-right-thought, the third eye, etc. They always say to trust your gut feeling because it is usually right. The problem is these days we haven't been able to remember what that gut feeling feels like, or what it is. It's like we're all turned off to it.

There were several steps I had taken to retune my gut feeling. First, I had to realize I had one and that took trusting myself and having confidence in myself, but to have that first I had to at least like myself, if not love myself and respect myself. In the past I had worn my heart on my sleeve beyond the loss of dignity. That had to end. Before our sever I didn't care, but after I relearned myself, I couldn't be that way anymore. I had a personal transformation just in getting to know myself and test myself.

Another factor was purification. How pure can one be when intoxicating and toxifying with various distilled spirits and natural mind-altering and exploratory medicines?

However, from the onset, I had received messages that told me how to safeguard, or at least stave off the gravest consequences of man's dissent into trust in big government, Federal government. To allow subsidiary corporations to pawn off chemicals more complex and medicinal on entire populations was a topic presented to me in my daily searches of alternative news sites and random internet sources, which led to credible information from learned and independent scientists and doctors who bucked the current of our existing social-political paradigm. Some chemicals we'd been fed affected certain glands in the body that helped develop the mind and the area of the brain that aided in using that "gut feeling." Either way, my diet consisted of only purified water—drinking and cooking. Cleaning and bathing was another issue. Naturally, in this world of perpetual unnaturalness, one could only do so much to guard themselves from the poisons of daily life. It had become practically impossible to stay away from impure, fake foods. I knew, having for a time worked with a company specializing in groceries because I saw every product, searched every ingredient, researched, and learned. Yes, cleansing for me included food. Soon, alcohol became one of my only vices, though I happily partook in a slightly bloody steak every now and then. Either way, a purified system helped in tuning the sixth sense. The cleanse helped consciousness become more receptive and active. I guess in a way it had to do with being more aware. I've always been aware of my surroundings. As a writer that was always paramount, whether intended or not. I became aware to the point that even my consciousness had self-awareness. Being aware was a start.

Meditation was another tool I used, and a tool looked down on by a great number of the populace. It was a joke to most it seemed. Still, a growing number of people immersed in the secular and materialistic life recognized the benefits of meditation, whether traditional, guided, or yoga. When you remember everything is energy and so everything is connected you look at people and situations differently. It even becomes easier to believe that one could hear others' thoughts or move objects with the mind because the empty space is filled with particles that in reality are just an extension of us. Still, we are unable to do it, though I've had sober moments when I can swear to the grand creator I heard someone's thoughts. I had once met a girl who said she saw thought bubbles above people's heads and images and pictograms inside them that revealed to her the true nature of that individual. The thought bubbles didn't appear with everyone, she said, but usually as a warning or to glean some other substantive unspoken communication. I believe she was an acid head in middle school, but then wasn't sure. I didn't often trust gossip much as my gut. Perhaps this was a trait some people just became better at with age. Still, my clarity, when not intoxicated by alcohol, was sharp. Even now, intoxicated, I seemed to see clearly. I saw I was with someone special, and I was happy to have him back in my life.

8

I was awake, eyes agape, slightly twitchy. Energetic and pumped, my delirium was accentuated by the peppiness of the white. I had double-keyed each nostril generously, a serving I hadn't had in a single shot in a very long time. We'd rejoined our pairs at the roulette table and left, both parties up on their bets. There seemed to be great fortune among us, beginner's luck I supposed. Perhaps there was a charm to Neville and Gladys; perhaps altogether the odds favored us. Who knew? We didn't win a huge sum, but unexpected as it was, that's what made it nice. I had forgotten everything I thought about earlier, happy to be apart from that world, separate and undisparaged by the grim reality unbeknownst to the great majority. No matter how much that majority shrunk each day, the amount of plainly apathetic people numbered high enough to keep the majority. The demented bloodlines had done it, they'd won the info-war and had brainwashed the greater part of the developed world through their various and monopolized companies, all inbred, all fathered by the same ghoul. What kind of apocalypse would they bring? I could only speculate, though in sober moments I often thought if all the major religions of the world gave any evidence, and if their belief was strong enough, it was a safe bet they'd bring an apocalypse as Biblical as possible.

But, whatever the hell! As Neville said, we're in Vegas, and we were just gonna have fun. What I was looking for now was another foot-long, frozen adult beverage. They had all kinds of flavors in these stands all over the place. I mean, never mind that there were bars around every corner, and people drinking everywhere you looked—if one wasn't paying attention, totally imbibed by the marvels of the environment around you, you wouldn't even realize everyone around was getting buzzed on something, whether nicotine, alcohol or the friendly herb. Yes, I smelled that in the air, too. I briefly wondered about Nevada marijuana laws. I heard they had made it legal to possess marijuana, but illegal to sell or acquire. What kind of sense did that make? My brain knotted. Bah! I dismissed the thought. Everyone was having a good time. I suppose anyone not was probably a local, or some fooled family that brought their children along to see the work force of Mexican people flipping 'nudie' cards at any man or boy they came across. Even *abuelita* was out there peddling smut and pimping young women to any taker. Still, if you were burdened with bringing children to Las Vegas, if you were a child seeing giant lions and roller coasters coming out of New York City looking buildings and a giant glass pyramid and a Disney Land Castle, you'd be so distracted—you wouldn't realize *everybody else around you was drunk or getting high on something*!

We gallivanted the ritz out of the Cosmopolitan, its jaja elegance and sparkling hip resonance ensconced in our alcohol addled minds, our streaked brains and avasted hearts. I was glad Neville wasn't so rich he was beyond the walk. I enjoyed walking the Strip day or night—though admittedly I've partaken of enough of the devil's drink to not truly remember the Strip by the time the sun set. We zigzagged south dodging cars and palm trees. Neville was distracted at a strip of discount shops. Neville was definitely a car guy and was drawn to a set of twin Mustangs, suped up and tricked out. Very sleek and only slightly less obnoxious than the pimped out Cadillac convertible with the plush purple interior and boa-lined backseat. These cars were for rent. Neville argued the rates were murder and that he'd just as soon buy the car. And he could, too. Gladys was a mess trying to balance all her bags and her huge Gucci purse and her foot-long margarita, all balanced on four-inch platform stilettos. There were only a few things remiss about a girl of her stature and gaudiness walking into a discount gift shop with an armful of Gucci and Prada, Dior and Versace. It meant nothing to Gladys. Just yesterday purchasing at ninety-nine-cent shops like this was life.

"Nevy, can we go back to the hotel; I need to put these bags down. My feet are killing me. I need to change my shoes." Gladys walked out of the discount store. Neville and Raoul were lost in the two-for-one T-shirts and fifty-cent shot glasses. I followed Gladys. She moved pretty fast for someone in stilettos. When I caught up to her I offered to help with the bags. She was more than obliged. After I'd grabbed all but one, a brick-sized Tiffany's bag, she smiled and reached into her bag and pulled something out and swiftly handed it to me. It was money. A Franklin.

"Huh?" I asked.

She giggled and replied, "Here, just take it. Thanks for offering to help. Neville will catch up with us. Let's go. My feet are killing me." We walked back up the strip to PH; it wasn't too far down.

"Where ya' goin'?" Neville yelled from back at the souvenir shop. We were already a block away. People looked up briefly at the distraction and then returned to their private world. We both turned.

"I gotta' put these bags up!" Gladys yelled. She turned to me, "I swear I'm goina' fall in these heels."

Neville and Raoul followed us a few yards behind, dodging tourists and looking around, snapping photos. I could see the Paris balloon ahead of us, and the faux Eiffel tower. The Gucci and Prada stores Gladys had ravaged were now across the thoroughfare and PH was right before us. The entrance at the front took us through a bunch of shops and eateries. The Miracle Mile Shops it was called. People everywhere were touristing and drinking and window shopping. A drunken jock, probably hours into his twenty-first birthday sloshed forward, his balance skewed probably by too many beers and tequila shots. The man who was no doubt his father walked paces ahead of him, embarrassed by his son's inability to maintain his drink. C'mon, dad, you gotta show your son how it's done! Don't leave him stoned drunk at sea, don't let him crash and sink—that's a beautiful mug you bore there, don't let him ruin it because you didn't want people to see you with your drunk son! I stopped by a drink stand to refill my frozen beverage. Gladys waited still working on her own drink. Raoul and Neville caught up to us.

"Are we going to the rooms?" he asked.

"Yes, baby, we're just waiting to get another drink."

"How do we get there?"

"I don't know," I answered, "I think we have to go through the casino." I wobbled a little. "I'm gonna get the High Octane."

"You are gonna be drunk," Raoul chided.

"I actually can't believe I'm still standing. Everything I've been on." I didn't realize I was already in front of the server.

"Refill, please, High Octane, Hawaiian mix, please."

"Extra shot?"

"You know it."

*   *   *

I handed Gladys' bags off to Neville before we parted ways. We went to our own separate suites. Raoul and I were excited as we rushed drunkenly down the modern dim hallways. The suites were at the ends of the long corridors guarded by huge, black double doors. Our suite overlooked the Strip. We could clearly see the Eiffel Tower and balloon and across the boulevard to the Bellagio lake and fountains. The suite was spacious, modern, and very expensive, everything colored-coordinated in reds, whites, blacks, and grays. Marilyn's famous white gown stood framed in a lighted shadowbox display on the wall with photographs of the iconic image that made the dress famous. Marilyn paraphernalia accented the room. I looked around the living space. I heard Raoul in the other room. He came through the door. He was shirtless and he was unbuttoning his jeans. He looked at me smiling. I sipped my drink and put it down, readying to embrace him. He was coming fast. He was in his briefs before I knew it, his body heavy as he kissed me. I gripped his thigh beneath his buttock, his flesh was warm and limber. I gripped tighter. He moaned, his mouth on mine, our tongues caressing each other, our eyes closed. My shirt was off, his fingers kneading at my hairy pectorals. We landed on the couch, a writhing of arms and legs, and gyrating hips. We made love as the fountains danced on the strip below.

*   *   *

We lay there, Raoul on top of me, I caressed his back with my hand, the both of us satisfied. I was a little dizzy; sweaty, I felt like I burnt off some of the alcohol. Raoul had been hot and aggressive. He worked me out good, but I had done the same, fueled rather than slowed by the alcohol coursing through my veins. Raoul was my idyllic prince. Every molecule of my body was attentive when he was around. They always were. It was like a subconscious longing in my DNA. I relished his skin against mine, my soul pleased to be so close to his, our auric fields touching and merging. My spirit had yearned for him when he was gone. The memory of his soul had left an imprint on mine. That imprint was a

[43]

deep shadow often hollow or filled with knots in my throat and sudden blurred vision. No more. I pulled myself away from that. I embraced Raoul. He embraced back. We lay there for countless minutes, comfortable, listening to the buzzing silence of the suite as the sunset began to cast a golden orange glow on the Las Vegas Strip outside.

I looked to Raoul. "I'm so glad to be here with you," I said.

He breathed deeply, "Me, too." He said. He looked up, lifting his head from my chest and we kissed again. I relished his soft lips momentarily.

"I can't believe how much partying we've done. Gladys is crazy."

"Yeah." Raoul buried his face in my chest and moved to my under arm. He inhaled and nuzzled closer. I pulled back afraid he'd choke on any of my body stinks. Plus it tickled. We laughed. "She's been giving you the white, too, hasn't she?"

"You know I can't down that many margaritas and still be standing otherwise." I laughed and looked at him again. "Are you all right?"

"Yeah." He looked at me, a fire in his eyes. Was it mischief? "It's okay—after all, we're on vacation."

"Yeah. I just wonder if Neville is aware of it." There was a pause. Both Raoul and I knew Neville had issues with Gladys and hard drugs in the past, although to Neville's discredit, he did enjoy dancing with the White Lady from time to time. Let the record show, if the reader hasn't figured, that all parties included didn't believe marijuana was a drug. Marijuana was an herb, occurring naturally in nature without need of manufacturing of any type. The human body was even equipped with cannabinoid receptors which meant the body was intended to receive the herb. No, the harder drugs were things like cocaine, meth, acid, and the likes. Gladys once went through an extremely dark period of addiction, though mostly on a substance called ice, which was a form of crystal meth.

Once Neville even asked we tell him if we knew of her using. She'd promised and broken her promise in the past several times.

"Well, I can tell you, winning a couple million dollars is definitely not gonna help the habit," Raoul chimed in.

"They'll snort it all away," I said.

"Bobby and Whitney."

9

I know this world is hard. But it is good. It can be better, but *we* have to be better to make it better. When was it that we decided to accept cynicism and sarcasm and an overall negative outlook on life as a country? As a race? My perspective was limited, of course, but you could see it in daily life if you chose to be aware. If you rode on the energies, you could be aware of anything. It took me sometime to realize these things. There was a period of time I was still driven by the baser natures, the heavier energies. I believed energies attracted like energies, so all I had to do was look around to realize where I was. All I had to do was look at the people I surrounded myself with, the situations I found myself in. I could not see things of a higher energy. I would not see them until I had changed my energy. For a time it seemed I would never see again. When one acts or thinks a certain way long enough they eventually become that way. The body and mind and personality could be re-programmed as it were through practice and habit as much as anything else. You just had to be aware of it. One day I became aware of my cynicism and the negative forces it brought with it: hate, depression, hopelessness, sarcasm, anger and the most deadly of all, apathy. I desperately needed to disconnect from that, for I had fallen into a world of eternal moonlight and become immersed in the vanquished sky behind it. I did not want to be vanquished. I did not want nothingness, so I lightened up and found a way to ride on higher energies. It started with practicing gratuity and letting go of the past and accepting all those around me for who they were. I eventually found my happiness. Travel made me happy. I traveled much as I could for a blue-collared writer, and followed the gravity centers that beckoned my soul.

There was a draw to Las Vegas I enjoyed. Something about being able to walk around everywhere with a drink in hand was very appealing to me. It allowed me to experience life the way I wanted to—slightly intoxicated. There was never a rhyme or reason to it. Innate in my conception was just that way of being. Theories I surmise come to the surface at times, but I can't be sure to trust the average heart, much less the average mind. "This is beyond your experience," child, but still you are afraid. Even the evil can be enlightened. And in such enlightenment they can parade, they can repent and recompense, they could agitate and take to newer levels the depth of the wayward. "I am your father, born of light turned to dark, turned to light again." The parables always take us into the forest and bring us into the light—not the meadows or the oceans, but pure intoxicating light. And that is what this was: a fun time, idealized and romanticized and for no fool to criticize. The essence of this journey lay in the discovery of the core and reoccurrence of the indomitable will of man to be free and to recapture the dignity of enlightened means and enlightened ways so as to subvert the malfeasance of this planet and dimension for in the heart of all resonant are the flames of compassion for goodwill to all.

Whoever said you were gonna come to Las Vegas and get your kidneys cut out and end up on ice in some two-penny, seedy hotel bathroom? I don't know. I know they said it. The Black Market has a good reason to exist in a place like Vegas. Where else could thugs and loan sharks sell human organs if their debtor is a couple grand in the hole with no means of repayment? That's a nightmare reserved for those who can't handle Vegas, and for those too scared to visit. Still, I'd never seen anything of the sort in all my time there. Usually it was men and women fighting. The female would be pissed at the male and his buddy for some reason and be so drunk and out of her head that she'd be screaming at them— smashed and livid with her breasts brimming over a thin black halter top, a skirt short to the thighs, a show for all the spectating pedestrians. Next thing you know she's trying to start a cat fight with them and instead they hop in their car and take off without her and she runs after them in the middle of the street drunk, crying and screaming. If it's not a scenario like that, then the girl might be passed out, stone cold from the boozing, and whatever else she may be into, and the boyfriend is going crazy looking for a phone, but nobody will help him because this is Vegas and the tourists, who've all been sold horror stories of theft and dishonesty on the Strip, don't know if they can trust. They are taught to be paranoid and fearful and untrusting and so they say their phone is dead, or they have no phone, which is a straight up lie because in this day and age, who doesn't have a phone? And I'm not judging. Trust me, I've been in these two situations at least once before, but that's on par with what I'd come to experience in a city like Vegas. There'd been no crazy mob stuff or missing friend *Hangover* type shenanigans. There'd only been boozing, drugging, and sexing. Still, you couldn't deny the history of the town. That's where all the kidnapping and black market stories came from, and the mob had been more than an influence on the city. Mischief could only travel so far in Vegas before wearing thin. You could take your shenanigans to all four corners of Vegas, but it didn't mean the whole place was like the Strip. I had some friends and associates who lived in Vegas, and they never had anything to complain about other than average theft and a downed economy, but a depressed economy went for everyone and everywhere at this point. Well, most of the world, anyway.

Raoul and I were heading down the corridors to meet Neville and Gladys for dinner. The hotel décor was minimal and modern with its own fabulous elegance, a hint that seemed more indulging with the slight buzz—most of the alcohol effects worked off in our passionate hours and reinvigorating shower. We had shared a half joint of fine hydroponic. Raoul had done an ace job hiding it from me, and I was surprised again at how engaged he'd become in the drug culture. I was also surprised he was partaking in Gladys' white sands, too. It was the effects of Sin City, I was sure. It even had me doing more than my usual, and my usual wasn't what it used to be. Looking and feeling as good as we did, being where we were, we couldn't help but to feel like somebody. Yes, I went to Las Vegas, and this was my story to tell.

The corridors were dim. At the elevator lobby we passed a portrait of a nubile Liza Minnelli, a vixen surrounded by hunkish men.

Neville's choice restaurant: something close to home as possible. He vied for the Tex Mex. One casual Cabo Wabo—well, I could do for some tequila. Dinner moved fast. Several shots, beers and margaritas all rolled into Neville's fastidious attitude for perfection, he having been in the service industry for several years himself. It was the only industry he could work in where money came under the table in cash. Most immigrants, illegal or not, took underhanded jobs. His mother, for instance, did homecare tasks and babysitting to supplement waitressing. Neville himself had been a waiter and proud of his service industry work. The lottery winnings only made the chip on his shoulder bigger, but not heavier for this titan. I wasn't too sure about Gladys' upbringing, but I do know both their families were from the same town in Mexico more than ten hours from the border, but as the niece of a coke dealer, I'm sure there was money there somewhere. I believe her family had been better off than Neville's back in Mexico. Like most Tex Mex and cantina-type restaurants in tourist-town, USA, the place was garishly colorful and festive. You realized, of course, if you actually went to any restaurant that was not in tourist-town, Mexico, they looked nothing like this and the mariachis were more likely to be singing a Spanish rendition of "Breakfast at Tiffany's" than a traditional Mexican *cuento*. Sure, maybe in Cancun or maybe even Baja you'd see a place like Cabo Wabo, but those joints were all franchised. The drinks were decent, and that's all I was really interested in in a good Mexican restaurant: a good Margarita or Mexican Martini. Sometimes I liked my margaritas bloody, as I did now, swirled in sangria. Today's mix was lethal when compared to all personal drinking history, but the coke would keep me from the blackout, awake to all Las Vegas had to offer. I didn't want to miss a thing, and prayed my kidneys would hold out.

10

Dinner ended abruptly when the manager came over and put a hold on our tab. We all had a few drinks each, a few rounds of shots. They had a special drink bowl that came with four straws; we had gone through two of those while taking turns in the bathroom keying cocaine out of an exhausted little baggy. We were loud and obnoxious; we were tourists in a tourist Tex-Mex restaurant on the most fabricated street in America. We were having a grand old time. We wanted to do karaoke, but the manager insisted we leave after Neville seized him by his tie and asked him if they sold Cabo Wabo sombreros in their gift shop. The manager was less than enchanted and just about called security before Gladys distracted Neville and paid the bill, plus left a hefty-tip.

We exited the establishment quickly and headed to the black and white tiled interior of the Miracle Mile shops. We were drunk, but lucid, all but Neville. He seemed to begin to drag and stumble a little. It was classic Neville, a total schmuck when boozed up. Before you knew it he'd be vomiting. Or crying. Or both. I walked next to him and tethered him by placing his arm across the back of my shoulders.

"What's up, buddy? How you doing?" I asked, mildly askew.

He hiccupped. "Not much, just enjoying Vegas." He looked at me and smiled, his eyes, though naturally oblong, looked like closed slits. "Damn, man, we've drank so much already for one day. When did we start?"

"Early," I replied. The alcohol vapor expelled from his esophagus, "Damn, man I feel dru—unk! I don't think I've gotten this drunk in a long time! Damn, man! Damn, Vegas!" He pumped his fist in the air, a true warrior.

"Well, you better get ready for tomorrow. We're going to a bottomless happy hour." I was unwavered, lucid enough to control. I felt a little shaky. My eyes felt wide open. I suddenly craved a joint.

Neville slowed down a bit and inspected me. "Why aren't you all fucked up? You drank a hell of a lot, too, and you haven't even blacked out yet! What the hell man, the old you would be kickin' down walls!"

"Ha. How do you know I'm not blacked out right now? Chances are I won't remember any of this tomorrow."

We walked along in that manner, pointing at the shops and eateries until Neville broke out into a coughing fit that resulted in him vomiting into a trashcan, scaring a family of four trying to enjoy a late night ice cream cone. The daughter cried as bits of spittle flung across her rocky road, vanishing into the chocolate. She looked quizzically at her mother, then her lip curled and she began to scream, throwing the ice cream at Neville, but missing and hitting the trashcan instead. Neville, thinking he was gonna get ice cream all over him, threw his arms up in defense and fell back, screaming at the top of his lungs. Gladys tried to calm him, but to no avail. The halls were marble and resonant, reverberated with his voice as he grabbed his ass and got up, still coughing, regurgitated *carne guisada* hanging on his cheek. I looked around only to see a handful of onlookers filming with their touch phones and video blog equipment. I laughed. A shirt in a window read, "What happens in Vegas, stays on the internet." Whether or not Neville remembered this moment, chances are he'd always be able to relive it.

Raoul and I left Gladys and Neville to each other and headed off hand in hand. We reached the exit of the Miracle Mile Shops, which was actually the entrance to the entire building. We walked out onto Las Vegas Boulevard, the crisp desert air filling our lungs. Before us stood the Bellagio fountains and the Paris Balloon and Eiffel Tower, as close to Paris as I'd ever get. It was dark out. The lights of the Vegas strip fluoresced and dazzled. I was lost in a buzz of sights and sounds. Horns honked, bells rang and whistles blew, car bass thumped, people chattered, card hustlers snapped and cracked their cards before passing them out. I pushed one away, nearly knocking him to the street. It was crowded. I could barely keep my balance. I felt Raoul's hand tighten in mine. I stopped. We decided to go across the street and catch the next fountain show at the Bellagio. Raoul had never seen such a thing. It was the most romantic part of Vegas, most likely. I mean, the rest was besmirched by sin and vice. The worst it usually got at the Bellagio fountains was a pair of drunks in mice costumes sitting around hoping to trade a few bucks for taking a picture. Regardless of the backdrop, it was quite easy to get lost in the fountain show. Tourists flocked from all over Vegas to come see the fountains. If you were in Vegas, you were bound to have the fountains on your to-do list, and if not you were gonna see them while on your way to do your to-do list. The best was at night, because lights were added to the fountains' sequence. They often played a song to it.

The crowd had gathered in front of a huge manmade reservoir that took up the expanse of the hotel casino. Here is where the show happened. People were lined up all along the wall, all the way up to the hotel itself, waiting for the show. Cars and limos entered and exited to one of the most lavish hotels on the strip.

Raoul stood at my side. We were almost center, the chatter of everyone around lost to us. At long last the lights came on and a hush followed by excited tones erupted from the crowd. Violins gently came on as the fountains came to life, dancing serenely like electric, gossamer plumes on the water surface.

"Con te Partiro." I whispered to Raoul.

"Huh?" he looked at me funnily. I looked Raoul in the eye, the universe hidden there somewhere. I pecked him quickly on the lips. I hope I never had to say goodbye to him again. Bocelli sang on.

Part
~
Two

11

The feeling of awakening snuggled and comfortable in a hotel: the crisp, fresh, conditioned air, the stillness of the room, the light peeking through the drawn curtains. Raoul and I lay with each other for a while, comfortable, only slightly groggy from the previous night. Our shenanigans hadn't been too spectacular, but that was a good thing. The last thing I wanted to do was wake up somewhere strange, or in jail. Or next to someone else. We embraced each other. We made love. We got ready and headed downstairs, phoning Neville and Gladys to see what they were up to. They were already at the Spice Market Buffet. We made our way to them, purchasing a twenty-four hour buffet pass since we had an early start. The best part about the buffet pass was it gave us the opportunity to try other buffets at other hotels.

The smell of bacon and coffee hung in the air. I loved the smell of bacon. I loved a breakfast buffet, though admittedly I hadn't been to a buffet in a while. It felt like I hadn't had breakfast in a while. My stomach growled. We grabbed our food from a plethora of stations. They had an egg station and a waffle station. I ordered three over-medium eggs because I couldn't stand runny whites in my eggs. Over easy eggs had too much mucus in them, and I didn't like that.

Neville and Gladys were off to the side. It was dim and certain pillars were made of lights which was cool. Everything looked new despite the fact the hotel had been opened for almost ten years since. The last remodel had been prior to 2007. I thought the look still held well.

"Hey, guys!" Gladys called. She seemed to be in high spirits. In front of her was a plate with one egg, two strips of bacon, and one sausage link. She had a cup of coffee, black.

"Dang, girl, not hungry?" I asked, blowing her a kiss. "How's the good ole Neville doing?"

"Hey, buddy, what's up?" Neville smiled. He seemed slightly flushed, but fresh and coherent.

"What brings you guys up so early?" I asked.

"Dude, it's like almost noon."

"Ha, yeah, I know. I thought for sure you'd be crashed. What time you guys get in?"

"After you ditched us?"

"Neville, you accosted a family and made a mortal enemy of a three-year-old." Neville smiled. "Do you remember? It's on the internet."

The four of us laughed. I gulped down from a huge glass of freshly squeezed orange juice. I didn't do coffee.

"Neville nearly fell down like five times last night," Gladys chimed in. "I thought I'd have to have security help me get him to the room." She laughed, poking at her sausage and sniffing. "You're crazy, baby." She reached over and squeezed his hand.

"Well, it's Vegas, babe," he said, jabbing into a thick cut of ham. "And as for getting up this early, like hell if I'm gonna miss out on this buffet and the twenty-four-hour deal. I can eat all day, hell yeah!" He nodded his head emphatically and shoved his ham into his mouth.

"Did you both get the buffet?" Raoul asked, "Cuz only one of you eating." He laughed.

Gladys looked at her plate. "I'm sure I'll be hungry later, once I've drank a little."

"In fact, can we get some mimosas here?"

Neville got up from the table without saying a thing and disappeared around the corner.

"So you've been dancing with the white lady so early, Miss Gladys?" I asked.

"How else you think I woke up this morning. Neville was up early and was ready to get out and do something. I was surprised; he was so trashed last night. He took off walking for a little while; I don't know where he went." She cut her sausage. "He was probably gambling." She ate a piece of the sausage, chewed it pensively and swallowed. "Uh, I don't think I can eat."

Raoul and I continued eating the entire time she spoke. I was hungry and the place was filling up. All the late risers from the all-night parties and orgies and one night stands—perhaps some of them hadn't even been to sleep—they were coming in droves now. But look, wait! Oh, no—here came the families, too, by the millions. Strollers, double strollers, Bermuda shorts, fanny packs, wheel chairs, booster seats. One began to doubt the morality of getting high so early in a scene like this. Gladys didn't care. She had been cutting a line of coke on a separate plate the whole time. A packet of sugar opened and spilled was her subterfuge should some unwanted pop up. She wouldn't need it for long anyway.

"Where do you keep getting that stuff?" I asked.

"Where do you think?" she said, swiftly moving and lowering her head and inhaling up the plate. She then poured the sugar in her coffee. She inhaled deeply several times.

"Girl, you getting dangerous," Raoul said, his eyes widened and nervous. He looked around, as did I.

"Oh, come on, guys, it'll be okay, no one cares around here."

"You're right to a point, but they have cameras everywhere in these places. Aside from that, if Gerry over there sees you and wants to tattle," I pointed at an elderly, bald man with jowls like a pitbull, "I don't think there is much he can do about it with his walker."

"Who's Gerry?" Raoul asked.

Neville came back to the table. He was followed by a waiter and tray cart that held two champagne bottles in an ice bucket, two carafes of orange juice, a chilled bottle of vodka, some glass flutes, and other server accoutrements.

"Wow, this is ridiculous." I said smiling. Everyone in the room was looking at us.

"It took a little prompting, but I was able to persuade them." Neville handed the server a Franklin.

"Mimosas, anyone?"

*   *   *

Some people liked to believe that god was dead. In a sense god with a big "G" was dead, but not god with a little "g." For instance, Neville and Gladys, both from devout Catholic families, were atheist. They didn't believe in anything. No higher source. Nothing. They still celebrated Christmas, though, because it was a tradition from childhood and involved family. Anything that involved family was a good enough reason for Neville to continually participate. He didn't need the religious aspect, though his mother and father still prayed to and thanked baby Jesus. There were still hundreds of millions of people who prayed to a god of some formal religion. I wasn't too convinced about the whole religious aspect, myself. I was aware there were obviously powers greater than mine that existed, and that idea alone was humbling, but a formal, organized religion just wasn't my thing. I always thought it was easier to reach your higher power one-on-one as opposed to a room full of people whom were of majority either apathetic or complacent. They only attended because it was all they

[60]

knew. I remember attending church as a child never fully understanding how it was that within the walls of a church we could all submit to this idea of perfect love and perfect forgiveness and compassion—all these qualities somehow inherent to worshipping a righteous god. For all we know, men like Jesus came to remind us how to behave, how to have perfect compassion and perfect love and forgiveness and humility, and to show us what our bodies could do if we had perfect bodies and full use of our brain (and by perfect, I don't mean "perfect" as "without blemish," I mean fully capable of functioning at the capacity the human body was designed to function). And these men (Jesus, Buddha, Mohammed, et al) went around reminding people these things, and those who had made themselves gods were pissed at them because they were teaching people that they didn't need these gods to connect with a higher source, they didn't need the church or the state. They could connect to the source, they could call it god if they wanted to, and that's why those who used religion, money, and government to control people had these messiahs killed or exiled. I especially felt a separation from these organizations because outside the walls of the church these spiritual people showed their true faces; they showed their true compassion which often was nil. God had become a jack-in-the-box that only came out on Sundays, when they dined at his table and he inspired them to compassion if they weren't asleep or daydreaming.

Neville and Gladys settled for chaos. They preferred guns to god as a means of salvation. Now that Neville had hit the jackpot, I was sure he'd stock up his arsenal. He had previously owned a couple of handguns and a Kalashnikov. I had never held a real gun until he let me hold his. It was kind of exhilarating, even though the gun was not loaded. Frankly, I was glad the gun was unloaded. Guns were another issue too taboo for Vegas, though Neville was interested in going to the range so prominently advertised all over town with a busty babe in a black tank top holding an Uzi of some sort in one hand and a semi-automatic rifle in the other. The only thing I really cared to know about guns, other than how to shoot one, was my right to own one, if not to protect myself, to feel secure in my person. Neville and Gladys were more into it than I. They even carried knives around. I never thought about it. I guess I took it for granted, but the black-handled Gerbers were there on their persons somewhere. The anarchistic prowess appealed to them, though they were usually a casual, trendy pair. The weirdness was bonafied by the now limitless access to their hearts' desires. The plushness of Gladys boot covers, for example, appealed to the masses as an expensive and high-end item. The montage of designers so eloquently clothing her left nothing more desired than to know where she held the knife, no doubt an accessory. She could easily be spotted for nouveau riche, but bless her soul, I'd do the same thing in her situation. Neville was looking more like a gangster in slick attire, though casual, semi-elegant. A black short-sleeved, collared shirt, black suspenders with white leather gripping, black slacks, a chain that dropped halfway down to his Stacy Adams shoes he'd brought along on the trip. He didn't do much clothes shopping far as I could see. That was all Gladys.

Neville and Gladys were a bit more certain of the direction they wanted to go in. They were interested in checking out some shops that had been set up as TV shows. They also wanted to go check out some of the celebrity spots, like at the Palms where some reality TV personality DJ'd. The likeliness of said DJ actually being in the building was slight, yet the allure of being able to say they were there pulled their desires that way. Las Vegas had become quite a treasure trove for reality television series. Yes, the future Aldous Huxley predicted where the masses would be entertained by the daily passions of real people in unimaginative scenarios had fallen upon us. Almost like a script. We, as a public, now found this to be our primary source of entertainment. I guess it could only be expected that people would not want to be fed scripted entertainment for too long. I could see how peering into the "real lives" of other "ordinary" people could be interesting. There was a series based out of a pawn shop (personally, I did enjoy watching that show because almost every item featured had an interesting history I always learned something from), there was another series that was based on renovating various antique items and collectibles, there was a show based on cars—buying and restoring, there was a show on making fish tanks, there was a show about rich house wives who most likely got a television series just because they had enough money to produce one, and, there was also a show on tattoos. The fact of the matter, however, is that it had become a joke, redundant and ubiquitous and gave individuals of no real merit the chance to shine in the spotlight. Perhaps it was that equalizing factor that people were drawn to. People loved it. Gladys and Neville loved it. I agreed to go with them to the pawn shop, but we wouldn't go until later because it was near the happy hour we had planned for the evening and that was on the other side of the Strip, north on the boulevard.

　　We decided instead to spend the afternoon at the pool. We walked around the casino a bit stopping here and there to pop a few bills into a slot machine or to bet on roulette. I was stuffed from breakfast. My head was only slightly a-spin from the Mimosas. We went through two bottles of champagne. I walked into the shops to pick up another foot long margarita and we went back to the room to change.

　　The pool was located just outside another check-in lobby area that was expansive and white, with loads of natural light pouring in through the long wall of windows. You could see the pool, which was already hosting swimmers and sunbathers, through the windows. The lobby was contemporary, with bold red-and-black pillars and accents. There was an oblong, translucent, acrylic bar. Day chairs lined the windows.

　　Outside, the pool was lined with pool chairs and palm trees.

[63]

Umbrellas and tents bordered the perimeter. A DJ booth and several bars were also present. Neville had rented a chic beach hut, draped with long white curtains and lined with sleek modern couches, a flat screen TV, a gaming console, a bucket with ice, a bucket with ice and champagne, a mini fridge with an assortment of intoxicants, goggles, and earplugs. The couches were comfy and firm with big tufted pillows. We sat sipping mixed drinks and enjoying the vibe. For once, my cares melted away. Born whole, I finally saw myself as whole, and felt content. I was happy just to sit there in my swim trunks, the pillows soft against my skin. Raoul sat next to me. His lime-green tank top hung off his slender shoulders. Neville and Gladys were drinking. Gladys was still taking the occasional bump, hidden behind the draping curtains. A DJ had begun playing so the ambience was loud, but muffled behind the drapes. No one noticed what any of us were doing, focused in their own reality, and I guess that is why Gladys was so casual. Neville didn't seem to mind. In the past he didn't want her to use. True, it was the harder stuff he was concerned about. The methadone. Neville had been a big coke user himself, but stopped without a seeming desire to partake. I was surprised when I saw him snort a line Gladys had made. Vegas must have gotten to him. Maybe it was his way of supporting her. I wondered how she told him, just because she'd been clean for so long. Neville keyed a small mound, some dust falling on the skin of his chest. Some of it sloped onto his trunks.

"Aw, shit." He said, picking it up with his fingers and licking.

"Someone's fiending!" I teased.

"Shut up!" he yelled. He hadn't done it in a long time, as far as I knew. "Now that I've eaten, I can have some. Because then I wouldn't eat nothing. Like you, babe."

"What? I had food." Gladys downed her alcoholic concoction. It looked like a Cape Cod.

[64]

"Surprised to see you dancing with the white lady again, Neville."

"She met me in Vegas. How could I say 'no?'" He looked at me, "And you, too?"

"Well, how could I say 'no?'" We laughed. "So, you guys enjoying yourself so far?"

"Yeah."

"It's beautiful here."

"I kinda feel like I'm dreaming, man," Neville mused. "I always told you. Didn't I?" He was laying back, his sunglasses hiding his eyes. "I always told you someday I'd be a badass. Now look at me." He raised opened arms in the air as if to challenge the heavens.

"You having a good time, Raoul?" I asked my lover looking over at him.

Raoul was slurping a frozen margarita—*where the heck'd he get that thing from?* "Yup!" he said. "Thank you, Nicky." He leaned over and kissed me on my smiling cheek. His lips were cold.

"Every man is king in Vegas," Neville said.

Raoul and I were the only ones not itching from the white dust, but the alcohol seemed endless. We eventually got to the pool and got some sun. The DJ continued his upbeat jam, and people drank and danced. There were excited shouts and laughter. The sun became too much for me; I retreated to the tent. The cozy confines provided refuge where I could lay out and dry out. I could have another beer. Raoul could find me, we could make out for a few minutes before interrupted by Gladys who'd come to bump up a few more times. She laughed at us, remarking how two guys together are so cute. We merely laughed back, kissed, embraced. We sat up, using our towels to hide our erections. We joined her in a bump. Our first of the day. It would help to level out the alcohol.

"I think we're gonna go back up-stairs," she said. "Neville wants to rest up before we go out for happy hour."

[65]

"You better be ready. He should probably eat something. I don't know if there is food there or not." I chugged my beer a bit.

"I want a joint," Raoul said. Gladys and I both looked at him.

"That's a good idea," Gladys said. "I have some in my room."

"We do, too."

"You guys are holding? You should have told me!" She smiled.

"I wish we could smoke out here." Raoul said with a fake pout.

"Oh, hell no!" I said wide-eyed. "The instant they catch a whiff of that there'd be hotel security everywhere. They'd probably take you away and kick you out."

"They'd take it for themselves." Gladys glared.

"Well." Raoul paused then looked at me. "Let's go upstairs."

12

Smoking a joint had been a ruse. Raoul was horny. He just about punched me when I asked Gladys if she wanted to join us. I looked at him funny, unused to his assertiveness. Neville came just in time and told Gladys he wanted to go to their room, so we promptly dismissed ourselves, grabbing another beer. We hustled through the cold glass lobby, passed the glowing crystal orbs that changed colors in the foyers, and to the elevators. Again, our towels came in handy as we were not the only ones riding the elevator; there was also a guy with really pretty eyes, and I guess two friends of his. Raoul stayed close to me. He'd just about ripped my trunks off by the time we got into the room. They were halfway down my ass, still moist, his hand fondling me mischievously while I tried fruitlessly to swipe the door card. Success at last, we pushed the heavy black door open, slammed it shut with our bodies, kissing deeply, breathing heavily. Raoul squeezed his body into mine, wrapping one of his legs around mine, opening himself up to me, my hands caressing downward, grabbed his firm buttock, squeezing. Raoul gasped, kissing up and down my neck. His penis was rigid against my belly. Mine was too against his. The warmth of his body just about pushed me over the edge. I had to control myself, not get over-excited. I picked him up. He wrapped both legs around me and I walked him over to the couch just passed a signed life-sized photo of Marilyn. We were a mix of flesh, I on top of him, he kissing and seizing me and biting my ear, gyrating into me, he breathed in my ear, "I want you in me."

*   *   *

What we started on the couch we finished on the soft carpet floor. We lay in spoons, holding each other. I had missed this intimacy for a long time. Grateful for it now, I released a gentle sigh. I inhaled the essence of my partner, felt the blades of his shoulders press into my chest, the firmness of his spine against my belly, the curve of his buttocks keeping me warm, our legs rooted together. I kissed him on the neck. He turned, looked at me, kissed me, nuzzled close and held me tight for a few minutes. Then he got up and walked over to the bedroom. He returned with a little pill tube. He was opening it as he walked toward me. He pulled out a plastic bag. I couldn't see what it was until he handed it to me.

"Here, you go, Nicky. Enjoy." He leaned over and kissed me again placing the golden top mushroom in the palm of my hand. I hadn't expected this type of psychedelics on our trip. *How pleasant,* I thought.

"Thanks, Raoul." I smiled at him, only slightly shocked. I popped the shroom in my mouth without ceremony.

I had a shroom like this before: white stemmed, white umbrella belly with golden gossamer cap. Very pretty, almost iridescent. Tasty, I thought. I had always been told when I first became interested in shrooms that they were disgusting to eat, and so it was best to make a tea of them or find some clever way to mask their flavor. The first time I tried shrooms they were laid fresh on hot pizza. It was quite delectable. The best way to have any shroom was to mix with weed. And so on many an occasion that is what I did. The effect brought out the visual aspect of the psychedelic, as opposed to the mental.

Raoul ate a shroom as well. Chewing, he made a sour face at

[68]

the taste of the fungus, but swallowed it down. I liked to hold mine beneath my tongue for a bit, to moisten it up before masticating. It would be about half an hour or so before the effect would kick in. Raoul had loaded a bowl of grass. I could smell the strong odor of skunk from across the way. It was good-smelling stuff. A close inspection revealed crystalized buds with purple-and-red hairs spangling the green like feathers. A beautiful specimen. We toked up, showered, got dressed, toked up again.

The world was awash in shades of gray. In this brief space of time everything was ambient and radiant with finite intonations of heaven, happiness, contentment, whatever pleasurable experience euphoric in presence presents the daydreams of life. The memories of lifetimes before crept at the corners of perception. Moments relived time and again. Here is the checkpoint to tell you you're on the right path. So I'm told among the myths of déjà vu and dream meanings the synchronicities in life are reassurances that you are where you need to be. And it flashes quickly like a dream. Like a place in your sleep that you are so sure you are there living, breathing, coexisting, and then shuddering awake in the darkness of the night, or with the breaking light of dawn cracking through your window, and the reality of the dream is gone. We toked again before leaving the suite. We were headed for our destiny. We were creatures of the moment. We were high on life in ways some would never understand. The point was to be beyond the reasonable faculties given by nature, enhanced in nature's course, the boundaries pushed to exceed the expectations that are repetitions masked by the veil of the cycles and smoke we cannot penetrate. I wanted to see the lines blur before my eyes and reveal the true nature of their existence. I understood, I thought. I felt I knew. I could handle the truth. I could connect the dots. I could comprehend its essence. I would know not just how to command reality, but what to command. But we were only just stepping into that point of man's existence. We'd been preparing for it our whole lives, though I'd probably be an old man before we saw signs of the first evolved humans, what I also felt would be a future incarnation. Still, I could not see. I did not know the truth beyond what my gut told me. As we walked the corridors away from our suite, the dim halls seemed to buzz and pixelate becoming dark animated grid patterns of gray and black. The circular matte light fixtures dim became bright portals of light.

"I think we are falling into a star," I said. Raoul was beside me, I thought, though I had forgotten about him. I could only look ahead. I heard breathing, and a buzzing sound that was intense enough to continuously intrude my aural field. A deep and urgent voice rang, "Hey, where you going?" I couldn't turn around. I looked to the walls, their lines pulsing in riveting motions, up and down, like some sort of vibrating electronic mesh. Gridlines and the portal. I looked at the portal. The star shined brightly through it. I was almost enraptured by it. I put my eye to the window. I could not see the stars or space through the portal, but the radiant body of the star. It glowed warmly. It engulfed my vision. I was falling into the body of a star. I suddenly felt its heat on my brow.

"We must be right in it!" I yelled.

"Nick!" I heard a voice coming from behind me somewhere. "Nick!"

The portal started to open, and then there was the suction of space. The gravity pulled at me. My heart began to race a bit. I had to fight the gravity. I pulled back. A hand grabbed my shoulder, helping me pull away from the aperture.

"Nick, what on earth are you doing?" It was Raoul. The hallway had become dim again, but seemed somehow fake and calculated. Slowly matter became stable again. I was surprised to see Raoul, though I wasn't. I had had my face pressed up against the light fixture. I was embarrassed. "What the hell kind of shroom was that?"

"I didn't think it'd hit you that quick."

"It must have been the smoke." I chuckled. "Pretty good shit. Let's go." We continued down to the elevators, again passing the young Liza Minnelli upon exiting, she being naughty in revealing black elegance, surrounded by a host of hunky men. Liza, that wild child. Were we ever in the right place at the right time. Her eyes followed us as we left the elevator foyer.

The casino was bustling. People hunched and slouched at slot machines, pushing button after button, smoking cigarettes. They leaned at roulette tables and craps tables, they were all so animated against fluorescent and blinking lights. The pillars of lights vibrated and pulsed. They seemed to breathe and shimmer. I felt like I was on an alien world of the future. This was a station of some sort, a nexus where people from various parts of the galaxies passed through.

"Do you want to go into the shops?" Raoul asked. He pulled me back to reality. My mind swiveled. I inhaled and looked at Raoul. He was gazing at the light pillars. His skin seemed to be breathing.

"Yeah, sure, let's do that. I need to get another margarita anyhow." I looked at Raoul. We had changed course through the casino, yet he still stared at the pillars. "They're breathing, aren't they?"

"Yeah, I can see the energy going up and down and up down. It's beautiful."

"Whoa!" he suddenly exclaimed and stepped back as if the roof were coming down on him.

"What is it?" I tried to see what he was seeing. The lights in the pillars seemed to stretch and connect then disconnect and rejoin up and down the column.

"Excuse me, sirs, is everything all right?" The voice was intrusive, but gentle.

"What?" I asked.

"Who said that?" Raoul asked.

"I don't know." I looked to my left, there was no one there. I looked to my right, there was no one there.

"Nobody, I guess. It must have been our imaginations."

There was a sharp clearing of a throat. This time I was certain it came from behind us. I turned around. A gentleman with an expansive brow and left nostril stood there. The nostril pulsated like an exposed heart. His mustache seemed to snake with his breathing. He had a badge. I could not read the letters. They swirled around.

"Is everything all right, gentlemen?" he asked again. "I couldn't help notice your interest in our light fixtures."

"They're cool." Raoul said, staring at the pillars.

"Well, we were just leaving," I told the game attendant.

"Mmkay. You guys have a good one." He smiled smugly. His eye seemed to bulge.

"Thank you. Let's go, Raoul." We walked hastily toward the mall entrance where a huge round glowing bar stood. The bar walls were made of glass colored an iridescent turquoise. The turquoise gradually shifted to other colors of the rainbow, but I couldn't be too sure if this was natural, or a byproduct of the mushrooms. We didn't get our margaritas at that particular bar, though. We'd have to find it—the Fat Tuesday's bar; it was somewhere in the corridors before us.

We entered the fashion savvy mall of white walls and black tiled floors. My focus returned and I was aware, though a bit woozy headed. We had to make it to the margarita stand. Refills were directly to the left of the casino entrance. If we kept traveling left, I knew we'd find the stand. I never lost my sense of direction generally, though I had lost my car once or twice. We eventually found it. The glare on the floor tiles seemed to make them blend together becoming seamless patches of black and white. I felt like I was walking on a cow. I moved forward steadily through the shops. Some of the stores were big brand labels, others were specialty. Lit

[72]

signs, bright stores, the same materialistic things, some stuff more elegant than others, others touristy and passé, plenty of treats and snacks, but Fat Tuesday's was in a little food court area in the corner of two wings of the mall. The food court itself had a pentagonal pavilion with seating for customers to dine; the food court was also surrounded in a pentagonal mote of red tile. The bartender at this famed Fat Tuesday's, no doubt just another in a long line of frozen beverage jockeys, was super nice and always offered samples and reminded to get an extra shot—a floater served in a test tube planted upside down in the slush. The liquor never escaped the tube until you pulled it out. The storefronts blurred as we blitzed through the hallway, dodging other customers, though trying to maintain some sort of social distinction, some sort of elegance in our stride—what was the rush? Fat Tuesdays would never run out of drink! They had enough booze and slush to last lifetimes, and we would see how many of those lifetimes we could go through before we ran out. People were seated at tables eating and slurping their drinks. Lobster macaroni and a twelve-inch margarita. Burgers and 100-proof wheat grain liquor a la carte. The wait was over. I got my sample. Pina Colada, a great flavor, but not exactly what I was looking for. Perhaps this time I would take a mix. Blue Hurricane with Rum Punch? That sounded delightful. An extra shot of rum? Why not? It's only a buck. Raul got a drink, too. He got the Blue Hurricane and the Jaeger Bomb. I thought him brave. The best way to shroom was with a mix. Shrooms could go in different directions. Either a mental trip is induced that comes in waves of emotion dependent on the user, or you could get the visual trip, most easily brought on by mixing. Raoul's brown and blue swirled drink looked like a scepter of opal and amber. Behind him people walked back and forth, the center of the pavilion becoming a black mirror. The lighting seemed to change in the room. Everything became more crisp and defined. The details of my environment seemed to magnify: conversations about corned

[73]

feet and aching bunions, schemes for gambling, the latest celebrity gossip and sightings on the Strip, the number of brides counted on their visit to the Strip, not enough lobster in the lobster macaroni; the way the earth seemed to pull away and push on the heels of the people on the mirror-black ground; the vibrant violet indigo sign radiating above the Fat Tuesday counter. Then the red tile of the food court started to change. It appeared to be a solid liquid, like drying red paint. It was like blood. I looked at the bottom of my shoe only to see paint smeared all over it. It dripped back to the floor. I looked at Raoul who simply sipped his drink nodding like a slow motion bobblehead toy, straw going up and down, his scepter slowly vanishing as he sucked away at the slush. He suddenly grabbed his head in pain, giving me a start.

"Ah!" he exclaimed. "Brain freeze!" He must have been loud, because the slush jockeys stopped and looked, as did their customers. The food court seemed to go silent. "Damn." He continued, pressing his fingers to his temple and slightly doubling over. He held his drink in his free hand. "I shouldn't have drank that so fast." He paused, "What's wrong with you?"

I looked at him and down at the floor. "Wet paint." I said, though there was a hint of a question in my voice.

"No wet paint." Raoul laughed. "Come on, let's go."

We walked away from Fat Tuesday's along the river of drying paint, there was no way around it for it divided the food court from the rest of the mall and no bridge had been provided. After a brief moment of hesitation and attempting to jump over the mote of blood, we walked on, continuing our adventure in the mall, when suddenly we were outside. We were still in the mall though. I saw all the shops and storefronts and the people still sauntering around shopping bag in hand. The storefronts though now had exterior construction, some looking like two-story buildings, and above that was a blue sky with rolling white clouds that formed and shaped as we walked on. I was mesmerized, but then remembered the illusion was just that. The designers of the mall had painted a sky on the ceiling, giving the feel of being outdoors. The clouds moved slowly overhead. We passed the pool lobby once again, its gleaming white floors and palm trees momentarily distracting me. Families and people wandered together, traipsing, herding in numbers sometimes tough to get around. We were fast movers, Raoul and I, a good match for me as I often left partners behind in walking, but it was natural. I wondered if we were walking too fast. Faces turned to look at us, almost rudely as if we were pushing them aside and they objected. More conversations stuck in the ear as did the trendy hip hop and contemporary mall music; I got lost in the stir of lights flashing, blinking, glittering, and glowing. It was all becoming a spectacle. I sipped my drink, the cold sweetness masking the stiff rum. I wanted out of the corridor. Hoped the end approached. How many times had I walked this very hall? Three, four times. It seemed I might have visited the place a little too often for someone so removed, but then again Cali wasn't so far, and the city wasn't out of my means. Still, driving wasn't always so enjoyable. I'd have to try train sometime.

The point of the matter was to make it to the happy hour. For some reason, I felt that wasn't going to happen. My projections were all off. Gladys and Neville seemed so far away, and they were, though within the same complex of Planet Hollywood Las Vegas. The spectacle of the hip, trendy casino, hotel, and shops had absorbed me deeper than before. The reality of my paranoia would normally excrete itself, but this time no security guard or camera proved threatening. I had seen the true nature of the beast, the way things were. There were no crimes too big in Vegas, as long as you weren't cheating the house and maintained some range of civility— after all, even a passed out drunk is civil in Vegas because the only commotion they may cause is occupying some Superstitious Joe's favorite slot machine. Security would wake them up and make sure they're okay, because to die would be extremely rude. Give the schmuck a bit of water. Make sure he can still walk. If he's a guest of the hotel, offer him a day spa the next morning, just try to keep your head on straight the rest of your trip and don't forget to hit those slots tomorrow. The first time I'd witnessed such a thing it caught me off guard. I had expected the cops to be involved, a citation for public intoxication, a night in the slammer to sleep it off the hard way. Even in a McDonald's once down old Fremont Street it only got as far as hotel security coming over and attempting to remove the intoxicated girl from the establishment. It was more for the customers than the actual drunk chick, but there was never any law enforcement. Even if a fight broke out, the security guards were the watchdogs of the place. They were more likely to escort the disturbance outside careless if the altercation continued so long as it was not inside the casino. This notion was comforting to me, but I had made it a point to never require a babysitter in Vegas. It was inevitable, the senseless plunge into the depths of something a bit edgier and exposed as a binge involving any type of illicit materials. For some reason this go round, the green flag waved authorizing a bout into different realms of intoxication, a means to an end, expulsion of life, but not in the manner that may first come to mind. Rather, its dissemination a more appropriate term: seedlings into saplings and the roots reach deeper as we go.

13

We had been due course for the Stratosphere north on the Strip, where most of the older Vegas legends still stood. Many classics had bitten the dust, quite literally, imploding throughout the decades to build the body of sleeker, newer, updated hotel casinos and resorts. The Dunes, The Sands, The Stardust, The Landmark, The Mint, The Sahara, and most recently, Fitzgerald's among many others, had all gone. Fitztgerald's though was only gone in name; the same building and architecture stood, the decorum had been all updated to remove that randy, Irish feel, and it was now rechristened "The D." Even Planet Hollywood had once been The Aladdin, and after several failed attempts to modernize and reopen the struggling hotel, the financiers finally sold it over to the owners of the Caesars properties. By the year 2000 much of old Vegas had vanished—the Riviera still remained, as the Plaza, even CircusCircus. Where The Stardust once stood, new construction had begun for a mega Asian-style resort, and across the street the Sahara was due to reopen in the next year or so as a brand new attraction on par with the Cosmopolitan called the SLS. I had stayed at the Sahara, ignorant to the history of the place, even in regards to mob rule. That story of Vegas was fresh to me, as I had only visited a few times in recent years. Safe to say that by the 1990s, most if not all the gang mob activity had been done away with. The mobsters taking residence in Sin City now were the banksters, the corporate monopolists. Who knows, they may have been the same people all along. Maybe Howard Hughes was a corporate monopolist, but what did I know anyway? The Sahara had been a nice joint. It was obviously older. The difference was distinct, the newer Vegas from the older. Nevertheless, there was elegance about the joint I enjoyed. It was subtle behind the age. The thematic natures of the casinos in Vegas were things always enjoyed. The vying competition garishly and bombastically displayed in a variety of ways. My rager at the Sahara seemed to be a memory of drunken walking down its long corridors of card tables and roulette tables, the central bar oblong and wooden, the bartenders chuckling up a Miller Light at three in the morning, their eyes peering into yours for just a second and stripping away a life time of secrets. It had closed shortly thereafter. Fresh to the place as I had been, in this new century I felt home as any place to the long forgotten shadows cast by the passage of time. It was spring then, there had been a hustle amid book readings and quick associations: a hop over to the Clark County library for a presentation and book fair, then over to a poetry reading at a local bookshop/coffee house. That was what I was there for on my initial visit to Las Vegas, and a particular reason for the brief engagement. I wasn't on vacation, though I took the same liberties as one on vacation. Security hadn't been as stringent on that visit, either. I never dealt with the airport's federally employed security, so flying up to that point hadn't been a problem. Flying private as I had for this trip had never crossed my mind. I had a couple of margaritas at an airport bar before my flight trying to decide what exactly it was I'd share with the audience, very uncertain as always what the audience would be like. You could never tell in a place like Vegas. I'd only experienced reading abroad so many times. Not enough to know with a certainty. The "distinguished" artist would suppose you should always know what the reaction of your audience is going to be, but I was not distinguished, and so preferred to gage the audience reaction in real time, to read their vibe and decide then whether or not I'd let it affect my performance. The readings had been well received, and I even sold a few books.

I visited Fremont Street the majority of the time then, on streets with the tourists and performers, margarita after margarita. Fremont, or the old drag, was in a world all its own far north of the strip, but an easy ride on the Deuce took you right to it. All types of people hung around Fremont. This was the place you were more apt to run into the homeless and vagrant individuals who sought out money or drinks from the tourists. More locals came out to play on Fremont Street. I was told one time of a group of young hustlers called the Trashcan Kids (they got the name for always hanging around trashcans), who were known for starting trouble with visitors. Once the fight was instigated and the victim was either distracted or on the floor, they'd rob the defeated party and vanish before security called the cops. The security guards knew who the Trashcan Kids were, had seen them a thousand times, could pick four out of five of them in a line-up, but the cops would never be called. They wouldn't respond to such a petty crime, not in Sin City, not in a town where as long as it wasn't too irrational, it was legal. So the Trashcan Kids would hang out. The trick was not to mind them, or the homeless that came up to you asking for a cigarette, some change or a drink. I always found myself inclined to share my drinks with the bums, figuring I was on vacation when I was in Las Vegas. Truthfully, knowing full well that I had plenty to drink even before the chilled foot-long margarita I held in my hand, there was some guilt involved. So why not share a bit of this, my three-foot chilled margarita beverage? It was a race to the end then, as humoring the less fortunate became awkward, and the bum couldn't figure when to take his exit, confused by unfamiliar niceties, and he says he has a hundred bucks and he needs you to go buy him some liquor because the shop keep is savvy to him and won't sell him an

[79]

ounce, and afraid he's now decided to rob you, you shoo him off like something less than human. You eye him but momentarily, feign compassion and continue with your drink, hastily imbibing so as to dodge the plight of another homeless seeking to take advantage of the kindness of strangers. Everything else is the bumping into tourists depending on the time of year and time of day. That spring had been fairly busy, and of course, all came out to Fremont to see the lights in the sky. I was often surprised things weren't crazier, but then again all drunken stories of Las Vegas are probably slightly embellished, if not induced by the storytellers themselves. I may have been the maddest one there, expecting some sort of Hunter Thompson reenactment of *Fear and Loathing in Las Vegas*. But these were not those times. We were nearly half a century passed that, and man seemed to only be exploring such legends. We were in the age of Gucci and Kim-fucking-Kardashian, the Palms and the Marquee, the Bellagio and the Cosmopolitan. The giants had moved south, congregating near the intersections of Tropicana and Las Vegas Boulevard. What the deserts first saw in the late 1940s and early 1950s was nothing like they saw now. The Hollywoodesque and Western themes had been traded in for the ultra-posh, and the extravagance of industry and fashion. You were more likely to get disappeared by a timeshare presentation than a desperate victim of some loan shark looking for kidneys to sell on the black market to repay his debt. All this excess, and all you had to do was remain within the boundaries of civility. And that meant not passing out on the bus.

*   *   *

"Sirs. Excuse me, sirs." The voice was faint and mechanical. It may have been a dream, some android addressing me through a menu at a fast food drive thru. "Sirs." There was another arousing; a wave of rabble resounded and it seemed discontent.

"Would someone wake those fools up. You can't sleep on the bus, and we're not going to move until they wake up. They been on the sleep back there for god knows how long. They disturbing the passengers."

"Hey, you need to get up." A hand wrangled my shoulder, instantly jolting me awake. I gasped. So did Raoul. Somewhere between margaritas, marijuana, and shrooms we'd passed out, our bodies suffering for rejuvenation.

"Thank you!" came the sound of the driver through the speaker on the second floor of the double-story bus. There was a cheering and hoopla. Half the crowd was drunk anyway. The bus driver had become their hero. "Now, gentlemen, I hope you understand, but the city of Las Vegas does not permit me to allow you to stay on this bus. I'm gonna have to ask you to exit now before we depart for our next stop." It sounded like a bunch of made-up dribble. He was calling us out in front of the entire bus, the passengers his audience. For a minute, I thought to call his bluff. Certainly he couldn't kick a paying rider from the bus for dozing off a bit, could he? I looked at Raoul and the people around us. They were all looking at us, a quaver in their eyes, anticipation retina deep. I realized they were all on his side.

"C'mon," I said to Raoul, grabbing his hand, "We'll catch the next bus." We stood up and I bowed my head defeated. The audience cheered for the hero, the bus driver, as he had overcome yet another obstacle on his daily route and evicted two drunkards who couldn't hold their own in the city of sin.

"Ya'll come back now," the bus driver called and drove off, leaving us in the dirt and litter of the south Las Vegas Strip. We were by the airport, near Mandalay Bay, almost exactly where we had begun. The sun was gone. Litter glittered on the ground. The lights of Vegas were in full motion. Raoul looked at his phone, grabbed my hand and began walking, and I willingly followed.

14

We were supposed to have met Gladys and Neville at the Stratosphere for a bottomless happy hour. We'd left the hotel high on shrooms and getting drunk on frozen beverages. Somewhere I lost track of time. The bottomless happy hour would be over in a half hour or so. There was no way we'd make it down on time, even if we took a cab. My head was stuffy. I looked at my phone. I'd received several text messages from Neville:

"Hey, guys heading over to the Strat. Did you wanna head out together?"

"Hey, guys heading to the Strat. Meet you there."

"Hey, we're here. Hurry up."

"Hey. Where you at? They got never-ending margaritas and beer."

"Where the hell you at? Answer phone!"

"*Pinche pendejos!* Get over here!"

"Fine. Forget it. Your loss."

We found our way into the Luxor Hotel, the obsidian pyramid that sat with slight austerity on the south end of the Strip. The entrance from the Strip was a bit awkward in finding, but we managed, passing a row of sphinxes and passing the guardian Anubis statues. The casino was bustling with the typical bells and whistles; muffled blues rock echoed from a live band playing near the bar. Sounds seemed to turn off and on automatically. In the center of the pyramid, near the check-in, it was silent as a tomb. The background music, some hip modern pop song was sucked through the vortex of the pyramid. The pinnacle of the pyramid climbed high. There was nothing but open air the entire way up. The rooms lined the pyramid walls, the floors themselves at an angle. I had seen a hotel with this type of idea before. The feat of this pyramid was harrowing to me. The rooms went up several stories, over twenty and edged out over open air. One who had a problem with heights would not fancy a stay as such. The energy was there, amid all the Egyptian architecture and mythology: sphinxes and obelisks, hieroglyphs and pharaohs. I could feel it. There was an exhibit on the human body and another on the Titanic. Posters of Carrot Top, now a mutated muscly potato with frazzled red hair and a mannequin face cut and pulled, stretched and filled. The dark and sexy Chris Angel hung about as well. Raoul walked a few paces ahead of me. I was still uncertain what he was after or where he was headed. He seemed to be on a mission. We had slowed near the center of the pyramid, where a tall obelisk stood erect several feet above us. There were sitting areas around it, but we only lingered, absorbing the energy of the pyramid. There were many things to be said about pyramids. One that interested me was its ability to harness energy. Scientists in Russia, I had read, had done studies showing pyramids to have abilities to manipulate energy in such a way that it could provoke self-rejuvenation and even evolution. What a cosmic dance, I thought, that simple geometry could activate the atoms and molecules of matter in such a way. Of course, there was a school of thought that believed we'd always had this knowledge, but that we'd lost it somehow. Indeed, these were times when a vast remembrance was occurring, alongside a vast awakening. The fact of reality as it spoke to me: the system and society we'd built around ourselves was broken and was working against us. We have now awoken to this truth. What we remember, though, is a much deeper truth. It is a knowledge that is primary as our necessity to breathe oxygen while inhabiting these bodies. It's the truth about energies, what we are, where we come from, and probably a whole bunch of other things I hoped to learn as I went along. There was no saying though, and there was definitely no way of knowing, which made me wonder if I should even bother to try and understand, and then I remembered that it was that kind of thinking that had gotten us in trouble to begin with. My head spun a bit.

"C'mon, Nicky, let's go." Raoul tugged on my sleeve.

"Where're we going?" I asked gazing skyward beneath the obelisk.

"Well, I need to find a bathroom, and get another drink, I guess."

*   *   *

Now, it might have been mentioned that Raoul and I had been separate from each other for some time. He and I only reacquainted a few years ago. I'm happy he's been back in my life as I felt there was a gap without him. He was a best friend I fell in love with, and was fortunate enough he felt the same. Growing up, that had always seemed to be a risk. The threat of falling for a friend who may end up repulsed by the thought of his friend falling for him, and most commonly ostracizing him, always loomed as a young man and made for difficult friendships. The alternative was no friends, or to be the friendly Casanova with his flocking harem close behind him, protective and enchanted by his every wit and causation. That was not the case with Raoul. Raoul and I had first respect, if not fear of each other, and what looming possibility there could be between us. At least that's how it felt to me. It could have been, and probably was, something very different for him. Either way the gulf of time we spent apart from each other had changed both of us. He had been meek and mild. He still was in a way shy, quiet, but there was something radically changed about his inhibitions, his limitations. Perhaps having grown he'd just become confident in life, realizing life was his playground and what he made it. Or perhaps it was Vegas. The biggest difference was in daily life, away from a place like Sin City, where he would carry on drinking and doing drugs. Raoul was an innocent child, one who denied such exceptions and relied on a different pathology for his purpose in existence. Some would have called him a prude, though he wasn't unreasonably prudent. He didn't mind drugs being around, or excessive alcoholic consumption. He just chose not to partake, and drowned himself out somewhere else where the pretty things were, and aural reverberations were pleasing to his ear. I was the party animal living my youth hard and fast like any brazen juvenile. Our first connection was deep. I used to think our meeting may have sparked the journey I've taken in self-discovery, but it was actually our separation that was the catalyst; our initial union only shook the fault lines of remembrance. It took some time to realize that. It took longer to appreciate. I don't know why our lives were scripted in such a way. I could only imagine what all he did or went through during that time when we didn't speak. He had changed, though. Now he partook, and willingly—willfully. It was a fun, new side of him. I just wondered every now and then what made him snap, and then I realized he probably wondered the same about me. He probably wondered how I went from being an out-of-mind, drunken pothead who always ended up being a bit douchey and undignified, to a reserved drug addict of calm temperament and spiritual base. It was almost as if we'd changed roles, except for that drug addict part. What surprised me the most was the cocaine. He strongly opposed cocaine, and that was where he initially drew the line. We may have parted ways for the use of cocaine in the past, but now it seemed abundant. Again, away from the Strip and the land of excess and revelry the use wasn't as crazy—heavens no. If the reader thinks I could live my life in the haphazard and unforgiving manner presented thus far, I dare say there would be no author at this point to write these words. (That's not to say that some writers haven't lived an abundant life of excess through and through, but most likely by the time you read their words they were already rehabbed and sober and in the security of their home or personal writer's nook.) At home, there was the occasional snowstorm when Raoul would surprise me with a gram or two of white. I found I never was the one who initiated that use. I usually smoked some low-grade hydroponic or high-grade shake. But I sensed that change in him. Cocaine and other such substances were much more dangerous than the old marijuana; everyone knew that nobody had ever died from marijuana—not like cocaine or alcohol. These changes were what set the alarm off in me, but the surprise was always overcome by my racing, coked-up heart. And I tried not to think about it. This trip so far had proven to me his propensity to drugs, seemingly whichever kind came his way.

Currently, Raoul walked from the bathroom. We had both gone in and bumped a few more lines, he leaving the little baggie in the stall for me to find and take at my pleasure. We had to be careful, as there were others coming in and out of the bathroom. Raoul had been washing his hands next to some guy when I finished keying the white. I noticed the guy's *Discovery* Daft Punk shirt, which I thought was kind of cool. I felt a weird type of energy when I looked at them standing side by side. I handed the baggie to

Raoul in an inconspicuous pass, and walked toward the door. He walked back to the stall, so I waited outside while he bumped again.

"Do you want to get something to drink?" he asked, adjusting his pants, when he emerged five minutes later.

"Sure. Fat Tuesdays?"

"You know we should put some white in our drinks. It'd dissolve in no time."

*   *   *

I was buzzed and I was wired, completely aware of my surroundings in a fantastically lucid way. If I were looking at clarity from inside a fishbowl, it would be amplified enough to take up my span of vision. The bottomless happy hour had been from 5 to 9. We would have missed it even if we had taken the Deuce all the way back. Was there a point in heading north? We didn't think so. I texted Gladys and Neville apologies and told them I'd explain later over dinner or something, and that we were at the Luxor. We had been anyway, but had already sauntered our way through the mall and into Mandalay Bay. We were at the slots wasting time and money. It was fun. The newer slot machines were digital and animated as opposed to reels and levers. They were all computerized anyway, run by a microchip that spit out numbers and probabilities. They were programmed by the house for certain odds. These money guzzlers were a fun way to spend time, even for those jaded by the rush of Las Vegas. I inserted more bills into the machine. No slots took coins anymore. And none of them paid out in coins either. They printed little coupons you'd take to the cashier and then they'd pay you out. Of course there were pit bosses on the floor and change ladies who sometimes paid you on the spot. Twenty, forty, fifty bucks went easy. Raoul was on a winning streak for a sec, but as soon as the losses started, they shrank his winnings to mere change. Nothing worth cashing in. Modern electronic music, easy and hip with a provocative beat, sauntered from hidden speakers just above the din of bells and alarms. The clink of glasses sharp before the dinging slots, we'd downed three cocktails already (thanks to our observant cocktail waitress), and that was only because we'd finished our foot-long margaritas. If you ever wanted to get comped while gambling at a casino, always make sure you don't have a drink in hand already or they'll avoid you like the flu. Once we finished there we headed back through the mallway towards the Luxor. These casinos were connected so it wasn't necessary to go to the street. We refilled at the Fat Tuesdays just outside the Luxor, 150 Octane made with Everclear mixed with Pina Colada. The beverage jerk mixed it and almost twirled in a perfect red and yellow swirl. Raoul got a Margarita straight up with a tequila floater on top. My head was already swimming, but if not for the coke that kept me alert and aware, I'd probably be off my feet. I was surprised I hadn't blacked out yet.

We passed back through the pyramid-structured hotel, by the obelisk at its center, beyond the Titanic exhibit, up the stairs and to the exit to take the monorail to the Excalibur. I loved all these little conveniences that really made it seem like a theme park to me. We exited between the legs of the sphinx and towards another obelisk, the crisp Nevada night air rolling into me. I inhaled deeply. Oxygen flooded into my cells and tissue, it sped up the alcohol. I couldn't really feel my legs, but I knew they were there. Raoul looked at me with a silly grin.

"Are we gonna make it to the monorail?" he asked.

"We have to. We have to make it back to the hotel. Which hotel is it again?"

"PH, Nicky. We're staying at the PH. Lucky it's not far from here."

"Yeah, that's true."

"I swear if no one is on that monorail, I'm bumping it again."

[88]

"Do you see anyone?" I looked around. There was nobody. "Where is everyone?"

"Maybe we just missed a group or something."

"Must be. Are you really gonna' bump it? We could wait till we get to the castle."

"I don't know."

"They probably have cameras."

"Yeah."

The monorail shuttle swished by and hissed to a stop. There were people in the tram, some standing, some sitting. The doors wooshed open. Some people disembarked, a couple holding hands, a family with a child, clothes dirty with food stains. The family had no doubt done Italian cuisine, and quite probably went for ice cream afterwards. The child was bouncing up and down, smiling with its teeth gritted. It looked up at me carnivorously. We waited for a few more people to get off—an elderly couple and a lone young man with peach fuzz and stubble on his chin.

We entered the monorail caboose. A group of Asians were present and remained. Though I didn't want to assume they were tourists, if Raoul and I were, there wasn't any reason they couldn't have been. We sat across from them. An older male and female sat together, undoubtedly the parents or authority figures of the group. A girl, boy, and girl sat next to them. The boy was externally effeminate, which immediately perked my attention. I wasn't attracted to him per se, but was aware of family when I saw them. An Asian woman, a young woman, stood in front of them clinging to a pole, one of a set of poles placed for passengers to brace onto. I realized she was intoxicated when she began spinning in circles around the pole and gyrating on the pole in the clichéd stripper fashion, ejaculating about how fun her pole was and that she was gonna dance and sing and party! As the tram progressed towards the Excalibur I could feel Raoul and I swoon simultaneously, almost as if connected. I glanced at Raoul. He seemed to be enjoying the spectacle. He didn't notice me, or the parents looking back and forth between the girl and us, or the boy looking between the two of us and then looking down. The girls were preoccupied with the pole-dancer. After a minute of this, the monorail hissed once again to a stop. The doors slid open and the Asian family scuttled off quickly. The drunken daughter twirled in circles before almost hitting the wall towards the escalator. Her family moved to the elevator. We got off and took the escalator.

The Excalibur casino was expansive and wide, very central to all locations with restaurants and shops and points of interest and exits on the perimeter. In our current state it was quite easy to get lost.

"Okay, so which way is the exit to the street?" I asked.

"Does it go to the street?" Raoul asked.

"Which is the next hotel over?"

"I think New York-New York."

"Well, where the hell is the PH?"

"I don't know. You're supposed to know."

"Okay, wait. Let me collect myself." I put my hands to my temple in an attempt to keep my balance. The sounds and people, but most of all, the brightness of the joint, were making me dizzy. I gathered myself. "Okay. I know where to go."

We moved through the crowd. I always told people who didn't know where to go when they were driving to read the street signs. I would do the same though this seemed much more challenging than reading while driving. But if one could not read and drive at the same time, it was possible to question that one's driveability. That was that. We headed down a corridor that led to a bridge that would take us across the street safely, allowing traffic to pass below undeterred by hundreds of sober and intoxicated pedestrians. In an attempt to get us home easier, I headed toward the Tropicana Bridge so we'd at least be on the same side of the road as our hotel. I felt I had strategized accordingly, and knew

Raoul would appreciate the foresight. Once we'd crossed Las Vegas Boulevard, it was a simple cross over Tropicana Avenue, and we'd be a few blocks away. We approached the Excalibur Casino exit; there were a couple of shops and eateries that led into a long hallway. At the end of a long exiting corridor that led to the stone façade bridge that crossed Las Vegas Boulevard, an information stand and hosts stood gathered. The loopiness of a touch too much alcohol, the resonance of psychedelia skirting the physical landscape, the filter of pot that circulated in the blood and bloated lightly the natural light prevented the events to follow from relaying clearly into the inner cortex of my memory. We walked down the corridor. I noticed my surroundings, the posters and advertisements on the walls: "Meet Taco at Dick's" and "Ladies' Night at Thunder Down Under" bordered by flashing bulbs. The long corridor exited to the cross bridge. Figures stood toward the end. There was a strange tension in the air, like the oxygen had seized up. At the hostess stand I saw a supposed customer walked up and then there were bright flashes of light, milliseconds later the bangs of gunshots ruptured the sound barrier. People screamed. Raoul and I had no idea what was going on. Was this a show? Was it another dance off or flash mob? I couldn't say at first, until I noticed people either threw their bodies flat on the ground, or were fleeing in opposite directions. Raoul and I stood there. I noticed even the people in the gambling hall had in some cases left behind their hand and chips. A second shot resounded through the hall. People shrieked and screamed. The scene was very surreal. Tourists and employees were scurrying about in fear of death. The other hosts at the guest stand had dropped to the floor. The gunman had turned the gun on himself, it seemed and that was the end of that.

"Holy shit!" I said, still moving forward. Raoul grabbed my arm.

"Wait! Is it safe?" he asked. He trembled a bit.

"I don't know. It looks like the gunman shot himself." I

stopped moving and strained to look down the corridor. "Look, he's dead." We stared off to the distance. The other hosts at the stand seemed to be arguing or something over their dead colleague. People were beginning to stir, their curiosity overwhelming their fear. Soon the police would arrive. Security and what looked like hotel management had begun to gather as well, some of them rushed passed us, instructing us to go into the casino.

"I think we should go this way instead." I turned and went the other way. We would go through the north bridge. That would take us to New York-New York. I wasn't so sure how to feel. That was the first time I'd ever seen something like that. My heart palpitated a bit as if my cocaine high had returned. It was just adrenaline. I wondered if they would want an eyewitness account. It wasn't as if they had to find the killer. I'm sure the testimony of the other hosts tending the stand would suffice.

"But, Nicky, what if there's another gunman?"

"Another gunman? No, I don't think there's another one. Don't be silly." I looked at Raoul and put my arm around him. We were both obviously off our hopper.

"But terrorists!"

"There couldn't possibly be another gunman." I tried to be as reassuring as possible, "I mean, I don't think a terrorist would turn the gun on himself after killing only one victim. I mean it's not like it was a politician who just got shot." I stopped myself from rambling and looked Raoul in the eyes. Genuine concern welled up in them. "What that was right there was probably a personal vendetta or an estranged lover or something. Hell, for all we know someone was filming a movie! This is Vegas! Anything could happen!"

"Oh, yeah? Have you seen a double homicide before?"

"Well, no. I've seen fights and stuff. I saw a group mugging one time. One time some assholes wanted to start a fight with me. But, you know, it just didn't happen. You don't wanna start a fight with anyone here."

"Why's that?"

"Because they could be packing."

"Gun laws are that lax here?

"This is Nevada. Of course."

I stopped him and embraced him tightly, my hand caressing into the back of his head, his hair soft in my palm. "It will be okay. Come on. We'll go back to the hotel before anything else happens." I stiffened my arm around his shoulder, "Besides, the last thing we need is a bunch of sell-out badges snooping around our suite and stuff asking questions, and if we stay here that's exactly what'll happen."

"Alright."

New York-New York was seen only in passing. We walked by a towering Statue of Liberty made of jelly beans on the way across to the MGM Grand. By this time there were sirens and red and blue flashing lights that contrasted the usual glitz and glitter of the Vegas Strip. The police and ambulance lights had almost become stagnant, though. Everything was, for all things considered, just as it always was. Some people on the bridge stopped and looked across the way, curious of the commotion. Others were totally oblivious. Raoul and I walked across trying to be among those oblivious and drunken people, but I felt my aura had such a radiant glare of awareness we could have been singled out in any crowd. I was afraid the cops were following us, wondering why we'd left the scene of a crime. The hotel staff would review the hotel surveillance footage and point us out and watch us as we exited across Tropicana to New York-New York. They'd find us and ask us if we were involved in any way. Latent paranoia. We entered the MGM Grand, cutting across the Rainforest Café, sobering and sobering, not refilling our glasses. The MGM was a passing fashion as well. Through the grand gold foyer two ravaged individuals, dislocated from reality in our own right, turgid with fear and paranoia, mixed into a mass of people crowded around a boxing ring stationed in the center. We had to fight our way through. A golden lion statue sat on a pedestal in the center of the boxing ring, and a man in a tuxedo spoke into a microphone. A popular boxer from the lightweight division stood next to the announcer. People snapped pictures with cameras and cell phones, professional photographers alongside tourists and fans. I bumped into some guy who had a girl hoisted onto his shoulders nearly dropping her backwards into the swarm of people.

"Jesus Christ, it's packed."

"Who is that guy?"

"Paco Immanuel," I practically yelled among the cheering crowd. "Top contender and returning champion in the light weight division. The fight's next weekend. They must be doing all the promotional stuff now."

"Oh," Raul said. We bustled passed the crowd. Once we were out of the MGM Grand, we hurried down the boulevard and hustled along to our room at the PH. It was a long and highly toxic day. I wasn't sure what to do next. My nerves felt tender from a combination of things. Echoes of the gunshots reverberated on their tips. I didn't want to let it spoil my night.

"Maybe we should call the cops," Raoul suggested.

"Why would we do that?"

"Well, to tell them what we saw."

I felt for Raoul. I didn't want to seem insensitive, or worse apathetic, but I was sure the cops would have all the information they needed on the matter. It seemed like a closed case to me. Crazed gunman with a personal beef goes in shoots victim and shoots self. Open and closed. Neither of us had ever witnessed anything so violent. I didn't want it to taint my romance with Sin City, or Raoul's opinion of it. Now he could say this was a dangerous place with the experience to back it up.

"Let's go out again," I said.

"But we just got back to the hotel."

"I know, I was just thinking." I looked around the suite. It was still fairly kempt. "You know, if it hadn't been for Neville and Gladys, I'd probably never have stayed in this suite."

"Yeah, it's real nice, but you don't really stay in the room all that much, so you don't really need all this stuff."

"Too true." I agreed. "Nah, these rooms are for the people that come in and just gamble and stay at the casino. Maybe next time we'll throw a party."

"Yeah, or try something crazy."

"Crazy like what? We've been a walking pharmacy for the last two days."

"I don't want to go tomorrow."

"You see, we have to go out!"

"I know. But I don't know. I feel pretty out of it. We've done a lot today. I think I may be at my limit."

"At your limit? I was beginning to wonder if you had one." I laughed and kissed him on the forehead.

"Why don't we go out just for an hour or so. You know, have a night cap. Then we can come back and snuggle."

Raoul looked down at his phone, looking at the time I guessed. "I don't know. I feel kinda weird going out and partying after seeing two people die. It's like we're celebrating their death or something." That was something the old Raoul would have said. I was at a loss for words. "Look, if you wanna go, I'm cool with that. I'll just stay in and take a shower and warm up the bed for you." He moved close to me, half hugging me and placing his head against mine. Face to face. He did that whenever he wanted us to reach a compromise, which meant he really didn't want to go.

I hesitated, and then finally said, "I guess. But I really want you to come with me."

"Where you going to go?" he asked.

"Probably the Cosmo or something. You really should

come."

"Mmm, I'll pass." He kissed me on the lips then looked me in the eyes, "But you go."

"The Cosmo is right across the street." I felt a sense of departure. A ball of disappointment struggled to form in my throat. "I won't be far." I returned his kiss, his lips smooth and moist. We lingered for a minute. I opened my eyes; his eyes were closed. I started to feel aroused, but resisted the urge to rip our clothes off. The moment of low energy passed through me and was replaced by a feeling of love and elation. He'd be waiting for me when I got back, so I figured the best thing for me was to let him work out whatever emotions the shooting had brought up in him.

"I'm gonna shower real quickly and change." A singular joy, changing outfits between each outing had somehow become a personal habit of mine when on vacation. There was an additional bathroom in the master suite that didn't share the kitchen and living room space. I showered quickly and stepped into something black, a high-collared polo with polyester fiber mix, giving the top certain rigidity. White and silver accents fashionably muted the austerity of the black garment and made it easy to look at. The size and style of my shoes created a dapper effect that traveled up my fitted gray slacks.

I walked into the living room. Raoul hovered over the red coffee table in the center.

"Here," he said. You should have a little of this. "You'll enjoy your drinks more."

"What is it? More white?"

"Yeah, something like that." He smiled.

"What, you're not gonna smoke it are you?"

"Smoke it? No!" He had made a few lines on a sleek, glass shadow box that housed a signed autograph of Marilyn. "Trust me, you'll like it. It's just very pure compared to what I usually get. And it makes me horny for it like you wouldn't believe." He smiled devilishly and squeezed my junk with his free hand. I was amused. "Come on, sexy, it's the perfect way to end the night. It'll make sure you get home with a clear head." He still smiled and leaned in for a kiss. I grabbed the shadow box and kissed him, his lips still curved in a smile.

"I'll try it." I took Marilyn over to the table and sat it down. I noticed the baggy he'd served the white from. The contents didn't look like cocaine I'd seen before. It looked almost like tiny crystal rocks. "Where do you keep getting all this stuff?" I asked. The lines were of fine white powder like anything I'd seen before. They didn't look whiter or clearer or anything. They didn't sparkle, but Raoul seemed to think this was purer. He had cut one of the straws from his foot long drink to accommodate inhalation. There was a time before when the pain I felt was comparable. It was sharp and stabbed at the back of my nose and under my eyes like thousands of serrated knives. Tears welled up in my eye. I muttered a cry.

"Oh, my god! You did the whole thing didn't you?" Raoul asked. He seemed a bit excited. "I told you, it's stronger."

15

There were several places to go to at the Cosmopolitan resort and casino, but I wasn't interested in the club, or the pool club. I just wanted a drink in a quaint, modern, ultra-bar called Bond. Both the hip and hipsters mingled with the wealthy and the famous, none the wiser to status unless a neophyte or genuine outsider. I, always the genuine outsider, managed to blend with the hip, possibly wealthy. Surely anyone willing to stand at a bar of glorious sparkling LED centerpiece glass fixtures couldn't claim not to be, even as tourists of all types walked by to further sightseeing destinations of the Las Vegas Strip. They gazed at the bar and its shimmering lights. They gazed at the people at the bar. The fiber optic walls and LED mountings, the ladies dancing in the windows, the alien lights and shimmering glamour pulsing and exploding onto the Strip, the music thrumming in the background, people seated or standing, drink in hand. I only wanted a night cap, a final *how-do-you-do Las Vegas, for tomorrow we leave you*. Now I was oddly sober and wide awake. I didn't feel wired, though. I was merely clear and aware and in total control of myself. It was almost as if my every move had been premeditated, and so meditated, resulted in precision execution of my desires. I tried not to notice. My heart palpitated. The shimmering of the fiber optic wall fixtures and crystal like bar center piece were almost too much, but I enjoyed it nonetheless. I considered phoning Neville and Gladys. The excitement and paranoia of the shooting had left my mind for the time being, and it appeared as if no one in the bar was aware otherwise. I stood at the corner of the bar, never-minding the other people in the business suites and blazers, the women in evening attire and trendy party wear. The bar itself wasn't huge, and was situated off a walkway at the entrance through the Cosmopolitan. Though there was something rather plebian about a bar off the main exit to the Strip, no one in the bar seemed to mind. Everything inside the Cosmopolitan was nice that way. I debated what to drink at first, and then opted to drink what shared a name with the hotel and casino. It was perfect, a blush of cranberry juice mixed with vodka and triple sec, and a lemon zest spiral floating on a crystal skewer across the length of the glass. The sterile chill and tart tint of vodka mix passed smoothly between my lips and down. I sipped the martini, taking in the sites, contemplating Neville, wanting to talk with someone. I sipped the martini again, watching the bartenders mixing and shaking drinks. I sipped it again and the concoction was gone. A nice size shot for seventeen bucks. I would go to the bathroom before taking another drink. I pushed my glass forward on the bar, its shadow bouncing left to right against flashing back lights. I grabbed my phone from my pocket and began to text Neville. If the stuff Raoul had given me sobered me up much as it had, as well as revitalized everything about me, there was no way he wasn't as revitalized as I was. Horny or not, Raoul was destined to go out tonight. So I'd scoop him up after this and see if Neville and Gladys wanted to get late night munchies or gamble or sightsee or something. There'd been no four-alarm fires, or mass shootings, only a lethal Romeo and Juliet altercation, so Neville hadn't lost out yet. I felt a small flame in my lungs. I coughed it out. I walked to the bathroom where I was accosted by a man in a basketball jersey and oversized cargo shorts with a color to match the jersey's trim. It might have been Miami. He had a backwards cap, also color-coordinated, a scruffy bro beard and few

[99]

gold chains. He popped out at me as I entered the men's room, calling, "Hey, dude!"

I kept walking, as I had been texting and pretended not to notice. I avoided him just in time. I thought it might have been funny if he followed me in, though I guess he could have. I finished texting Neville, did my business, and walked back out only to find the guy was waiting outside, leaning against the wall. He came up to me immediately, his pants hanging low, his jersey hiding his underwear. He had tats and a couple gold teeth and rings.

"Hey, man, what's up?" He reached a hand out, approaching me quickly. "I know this is weird man, I don't mean no disrespect, but I just wanted to say you look sharp, man. I can really tell there's something different about you. You really caught my eye." He wasn't speaking so loud that everyone heard our conversation, but he was loud enough to get the message. His gravity pulled us toward the wall. I wondered if he was coming on to me. He didn't seem like the type and I definitely didn't get any type of homosexual vibe from him. I got another vibe from him.

"So what are you, visiting Vegas or something? You from around here?"

"Yeah, just here for the weekend."

"That's awesome dude. I can tell what you are. You gotta be an artist or something. What do you do? Do you do music?"

"No, no, I'm a writer. How about you?"

"Oh, nah, I'm just in town with my family. They staying here, so I'm staying with them. I live here, but I figure, long as they're visiting, I may as well come an' stay myself, you know. That way I don't gotta keep going back and forth into the city. Sides, I got comps, you know what I mean? I pay my dues. So you know, see a few shows with the folks, take'em out to eat. I got them a suite here, you know. Shit ain't cheap." I might have noted the bottled of Ciroc Vodka in his hand if I hadn't been so perplexed with the reason for his contact with me. He seemed to read me well, generally speaking.

"Yeah, I bet," I replied.

"So, listen, you're in town a few days. You need some party? I got some good shit." I looked at the guy. *Was I being hustled?* "What do you like to do?"

"I, me, I smoke usually."

"Dude, I got some good shit. Hydroponic shit. It's the best." I looked to him. He got closer to me. "Dude, you do white? I got some on me. If you want it now, I'll hook it up. Let's go try it."

"Try it? Where? Here?"

"Yeah, we'll just go into the bathroom. Trust me, it's good shit, man. I'll give you a sample."

"Well, what's the price, man?"

"I get you an 8-Ball for ninety bucks, man. Pure shit."

"No, I mean on the green."

"Oh. Dro. Hmm." He put his free hand to his chin, his other held tightly the Ciroc. "You know the reg, tweny a g, an 8th usually go for sixty around here, but I'll cut it to you for fifty-five."

"How about forty-five?"

He sucked the air in the through the corner of his mouth. "Man, that's kinda tight."

"Well, it's cool, dude. I got this friend in town. He's looking to hook me up. But thanks anyway."

"Well try the white, man. Come on." He put his arm around my shoulder. "Let's check it out. I'll give you a sample."

I was loosened a bit from the martini I drank, but I was still clear, and a bit annoyed by this hustler. I pushed his arm off.

"Look, man, I appreciate the compliments," I stepped away, "But, I'm good. Check ya later."

I turned and walked away as he called back at me, saying "*aaight*" or something to that nature. His tone sounded nonthreatening, if not somewhat disappointed. As I walked back to Bond I ran into two state trooper police officers. They were fit and looked very intimidating. I had never seen their type in the hotels. Usually it was casino security, and maybe a city cop or two, but typically not even that. They caught my attention because I was just about to consider a deal. They walked passed me in the direction I had just come from. I kept walking without looking back.

Once I made it back to Bond, the dazzling LED dancing and pulsating in this sleek, modern, ultra-lounge, I walked passed the bar around to the other side where the frenzy of lights and people would provide cover from the wannabe gangster-thug hustler hustling drugs outside casino bathrooms, and possibly the cops. Unaware of where I was at the bar I looked around, the far side, opposite corner. I was a bit closer to the lounge area. It was darker, and there was a DJ spinning discs, or perhaps Mp3, who knew. The LED wall fixtures were more prominent, and the LED glass centerpiece of the bar more focal because the proximity of the walls. There was a couple to my right and few barflies along the center and far end of the strip. To my left was a very good-looking guy with a Cosmopolitan in front of him. I ordered a vodka rocks and turned to him and said, "I had one of those earlier. Are you enjoying it?"

He smiled. He had a very cute smile.

"Yeah, it's pretty good. I've never had a Cosmo before."

"Well, so as long as you're at the Cosmo, you may as well have a Cosmopolitan." The two of us laughed.

"I'm Nick."

"My name's Mattie."

My vodka rocks arrived. I took a sip. It was smooth.

"So what brings you here, Mattie?" I looked him up and down as he spoke, trying not to be noticed. He was probably a little younger than me. He wore shorts that revealed firm, sculpted calves, and fitted all the way up to his swollen ass. His V-neck shirt hung off what was surely a well-toned body. I recognized his shoes as Stacy Adams sandals. There was a bit of style here, though he was roguishly underdressed for the ultra-lounge. To his benefit, he was wearing dark colors.

Mattie had explained how he was in town with his folks on vacation, and how they were staying in the Cosmopolitan. He said he was bored because his parents just go to shows and buffets and he has no one to hang out with. Further conversation revealed he was a college student from Austin, Texas, a fact that intrigued me because I once lived there. I felt his youthful beefiness well-represented the state. His smile was contagious as addictive. It made you wanna see it pout and moan in ecstasy. The bass pulsed. *Jesus Christ*, I thought, *I am getting horny.*

"So what are you doing in town?" he asked. "This is a cool bar, isn't it?"

"Yeah, it is," I replied, looking again at the lights and ignoring the bulge growing in my pants. I cleared my throat. I took a sip. "Well, officially I'm here on vacation, but I'm also writing a novel."

"A novel? Cool. What about?" He stepped a bit closer, finishing his Cosmopolitan.

"Well, it's only coming together. It's a spectral journey exploring the pathos of the American man in a time of great interest. I really couldn't say any more than that." And really that's all there was to it because I had only just decided I was writing a novel then and there. It made no difference to Mattie because I had writing credentials, and that's all I needed.

"So do you write anything else?"

"Poetry."

"Poetry?" He brightened. "Cool. I write poetry, too."

"Yeah, I've always been into it, though I'm sometimes shy about it." I paused. "Quite frankly, I don't know why I write poetry. I know I think the archetype of the poet is an interesting one. I think it is easier to say, 'I live poetry,' than to say I write poetry. Does that make sense?"

When I turned to Mattie he was ordering another drink. He was leaned over the bar to speak to the bartender over the music and crowd. I took a long hard look at his figure, his robust and taught curves; the way his shorts clung tightly to his bubbled ass. The bulge in my pants stiffened. I turned in time to hear him order, "A Jack Honey on the rocks, please." When I heard that, I thought I'd have an orgasm. That was one of my favorite spirits. He waited until the bartender served him. He paid in cash, tipping a dollar. I didn't think the bartender was amused; he certainly didn't look it. Mattie took a sip and inhaled deeply. He turned to me.

"Oh. You were saying? Do you have any poems memorized?"

"I wish I could, but I'm not that good." His eyes widened and he lifted his eyebrows. I smiled. For some reason the music sounded really good. The aural profundity was crisp and fit into every sonic nook and pore of the situation. It pulsated vibrantly. The colors began to pop out at me too with such clarity. Mattie looked pure beneath the shimmering white of the LED crystalline sculpture above the bar.

"You mean you don't have any poems memorized?"

"Not really. I'm more of an ink-and-paper poet."

"Oh, come on, you can at least try. There's got to be something."

I really wasn't one to quote my poetry. Not that I was coy about it, I mean I enjoyed reading out loud whenever I had the chance. "Okay, I'll try." I cleared my throat and closed my eyes. I thought for minute, then looked into his eyes and spoke,

"The beautiful clarity
moment to moment
shimmering crystalline in your eye
the daggers in your smile

[104]

dangerous just enough to tempt
close enough to want to dodge
pure enough to want to service
bouncing from one rainbow to another
wondering if you see what I see,
hoping you will know what I know."

I'd nothing memorized so had to make it up on the spot. I felt like a prostitute, and a cheesy one at that. Mattie seemed to like it. His jaw hung open. I reached over and placed my finger under his chin and closed his mouth. He looked at my finger and then up at me and slowly smiled. His eyes said something more though. There was a vortex in his eyes, a secret understanding. I could feel the electricity as I withdrew my hand. We both turned to face the bar. I kicked back the last of my vodka.

"That was really good," he said, and took another sip of his whiskey.

"Thanks," I said. I didn't know what else to say. We had had a penetrating moment, I was sure of it. I noticed he took a side step closer to me. We were now side by side.

"I really wish I could learn to write poetry like that. That sounded like real stuff, like you know kind of classic. Kind of mystic, if that makes any sense. Like you have to decipher the message of your language. Mine are more like confessional."
He was talking towards my ear. I leaned over slightly to listen.

"Confessional?"

"Yeah, you know, more straight forward." He leaned a little closer, "You really get the picture when you read my work. I don't like to leave anything to the imagination." He leaned closer, his eyes sparkling, his hand beneath the bar suddenly braced my crotch and squeezed my already throbbing member. He never flinched. "I'm direct and to the point."

I grabbed his drink and finished it for him. He smiled and started to laugh. "I like you," he said. "I think maybe you could teach me a lot of things." His hand was on my crotch still.

"Another drink, sirs?" The bartender's voice dissolved our private reality. He removed his hand.

"Two Long Islands, my tab, please."

"Coming right up."

"Mattie." I stepped in close to him, placed my hand flatly on his lower back like any bro would do. "As you can tell, you have given me a raging hard-on." I was extremely tempted to rub my hand over the curves of his ass that rolled beneath his thin cotton shorts. If we'd been at a gay bar, I'd probably have done it a long time ago. Then again, if we'd been at a gay bar, there'd probably have been five other johns around him already. But I didn't. There was another reason why I didn't, too. Raoul. "I'd like to teach you a lot of things." I squeezed the side of his stomach. It was firm and meaty. "But, to be honest, I'm on vacation with my boyfriend."

The bartender brought our Long Island Iced Teas. I thanked him and he turned away. I took a sip straight away. A good Long Island was made with a splash of cola and a good mix of spirits. I could taste the liquors. The gin stuck out, very zesty beneath the other liquors. It had been one of those nights that should have ended with me vomiting my guts out on the verge of passing out, having already been blacked out for the last few hours, and I wouldn't remember I was blacked out until the next day, which I thought a cruel exchange. But that wasn't the way that it was going. I could only guess what the gin would do. I stayed away from gin as much as possible. The closest I'd get is a Long Island, because at least there were three other hard liquors to balance it. You will never see me with a gin and tonic. I don't even think that it is because gin is too strong for me; it's just that it does terrible things to me. There's a story about it I'll tell you sometime. In the meantime, Mattie was pouting, but not the way I wanted him to.

"It's cool, Mattie. You're in Vegas, there's no telling what could happen." I smiled, patted his back, my hand again resting there and with my free hand raised my glass. "Cheers," I said.

"He raised his glass and our Long Islands clinked, "Cheers!" He smiled and took a long drag of his beverage. He picked up a napkin from the pulsing bar top and wiped his mouth. He leaned closer and put his arm around my shoulder so that our arms zigzagged behind each other's back, his above mine. He eyed his glass then looked at me. "This is a good drink. What do you call it?"

"It's a Long Island Iced Tea."

"There's tea in it?"

"No, it's soda."

He laughed. "So why do they call it a Long Island Iced Tea?" He smiled.

"I don't know." It was hard not to smile.

"You know I was thinking, maybe if your boyfriend was interested maybe we could all play together?"

"You really are to the point." I looked at him, perhaps a bit stunned. He lowered his arm around my shoulder, forcing my arm down. My hand rolled over the small of his back. He pushed my arm down till my palm rested on the upper curves of his ass. They were just as firm as I thought they'd be, and full. My hand rested there, until I moved it away and brought it back to its own comfort zone. My extremities tingled.

"I swear, Nicky," he called me Nicky with a half-pleading voice, "if I have to spend one more day with my parents without getting some dick, I'm going to kill myself!"

"Ok, Mattie, calm down," I hushed him up. I pondered the idea. Raoul did want to try different things, but I wasn't sure if he was averse to a *ménage a trois*. Mattie was a fine young man, I'm sure Raoul may find his delicacies desirable as well. I took a sip of my drink. Tried to stage a contemplative face. "Well, it couldn't hurt to ask. You can come to our suite at the PH."

[107]

"Oh, the PH. You're right across the street. How exciting!" Mattie smiled, took another long slug of his Long Island. These drinks could really pack a punch.

"Are you enjoying your Long Island?" I asked.

"Yeah, it's pretty good. Goes down smooth." He smiled.

"Yessir, wait till you get outside. It'll really get you then." I smiled back, sipping my drink again. "We'll finish these and then we can head back."

"Sure."

My phone buzzed in my pocket. It was Neville, he was messaging me back. He said not to worry about missing our happy hour drinking date and asked if we'd heard about the shooting at the Excalibur, to which I replied "*it's a long story.*" He said they were having a shindig at their suite and that we should head over. I knew there'd be something going on tonight. We'd go back to the suite, I'd introduce Raoul and Mattie and see if he'd wanna tie it on. We'd do that, go to the party, or vise-versa. I finished my drink, just as he. I called the bartender to close my tab and left an ample tip in cash. I grabbed Mattie's hand, not caring about the couples and groups of bros and business men staring, and we left the modern Technicolor spectacle of the elegant Bond ultra-lounge.

16

When we arrived at the suite I'd been away for a little over an hour. I was still right and awake, with a clarity that made me feel I'd just taken a fat line of coke, but I'd not had anything since I'd left. I'd certainly drank enough I should have wobbled some, but I didn't mind. Mattie was the one who wobbled as we left the Cosmopolitan. I had fun helping him balance, holding him up, feeling his body press against mine as we hobbled to the hotel. The air really did hit him, but he was able to compose himself just enough. I thought he may have been using his drunkenness as an excuse to make body contact. We used the crosswalk from Harmon Street to get across the Vegas Strip. There was a bit of a challenge using the stairs, and I continued to brace Mattie. The stairs were a bit secluded. Not many people were heading up and down them at that time. There Mattie stopped me and kissed me, running his hands up and down my back, moaning. His fingers dug into my back. We made out for a second, I allowing the alcohol to take me away. We stopped abruptly, just as our passion reached a boiling point and moved on down the walkway. We laughed and chatted a bit more. We had to enter through the mall to get to the Casino to get to the room elevators. Mattie liked the Miracle Mile, but loved the Caesar's Palace Forum Shoppes. As it was his first time in Vegas, he'd made it a point to check out all the fashionable consumer areas, and had already done damage to his checkbook, but with joy. By the time we'd reached the casino he'd started walking straight, to the point that I didn't have to brace him. We'd also stopped holding hands just because we didn't care to draw attention to ourselves in public. Interestingly enough about Las Vegas, it did offer some relevancies for the alternative lifestyle, but on the Strip, "acting out" was frequently terminated by security and hotel staff. The pole was reserved only for women to dance on, they'd say. They'd discourage public displays of affection while handing out pimp business cards to every swinging dick that walked by. There had even been cases of violence against openly flamboyant males. We didn't have to worry about that, though as good as we looked together, people may have assumed we were lovers.

When we arrived at my room I walked in the door, gripping the silver door knob and pushing its heavy, black body. Mattie followed behind me. He made "ooh's" and "ah's" as he looked around at our suite. "Pretty sweet," he said. I looked at him ironically. There was no sign of Raoul. His backpack sat open on the sofa, but I didn't see him. His junk was still on the table, too, but the baggy was noticeably depleted.

"Hang on a moment while I look for Raoul." I walked through the living room towards the master bedroom. The door was shut. When I opened the door I noticed the lights were on and heard muffled grunting coming from within. Raoul was standing at the edge of the bed with his pants around his ankles. Some guy I didn't know was behind him rhythmically grinding into Raoul's exposed ass, holding his shirt up to the nape of his neck, gripping his shoulder, reaching around with his other hand, rhythmically jerking at Raoul's cock. On the bed was another guy standing holding Raoul's head as Raoul swallowed deeply the stranger's penis. He was holding Raoul's head right on his ears. Raoul never heard me coming, but I heard him and watched him before he turned and saw me standing there. I couldn't say anything. My stomach had knotted deeply, my heart froze.

"Nicky!" he pushed the guy off him from behind who had still been jerking him off, he quivered from tender nerves, and came after me. Unsure of what exactly I was going to do, I had retreated to the living room and to the kitchen where I had found Mattie. He looked surprised to see me.

"Nick, let me explain!" Raoul's voice came from somewhere behind me.

"Explain!?" I fumed. "What are you going to explain?"

Nick entered the room. He had pulled his pants up, his shirt and hair were disheveled. He had a look of shame on his face. He had tears welling in his eyes. Then he saw Mattie, who was wide eyed in awkwardness. "Who's that?" Raoul spat.

"Who's this? Who are they?" I pointed to the room. Raoul glanced in that direction looking down.

"Look, Nick, I can explain everything."

"There's nothing to explain Raoul," I felt like I was choking, "I see who you are now, that's all. And that's fine."

"No, Nick, it's not like that."

When Raoul and I had first been with each other, there had been those moments of uncertainty, moments of jealous, petty or otherwise. I had even accused him of being sexually involved with others while we were in a relationship. He'd always denied it, even became fiercely upset at such claims. These were things I had to push behind me. By the time we'd started talking to each other again, they were long buried, a subject matter of the deep past that had no relevance to us in the present. My gut churned.

"Look, Raoul." I felt the warmth creep up into my face as a lump welled in my throat. I didn't want to be this way on vacation. I didn't want our time together to be like this. "We've been through a lot, and I don't know that I want to go through this again."

"What do you mean again? I've never—" He stopped in midsentence, "You still think I cheated on you, don't you? You're the one that was always horny for other boys. I would never do something like that to you."

"You just did, Raoul!" There was silence. Mattie just stood and stared between the two of us. I looked down, "You should know I've never cheated on you, not even back then. Not even no matter how many guys came around and flirted with me. The past is behind us Raoul. It means nothing to me. But now, here, you are in our own suite! That changes everything."

The memories of our previous relationship were stirring in me. I had killed most those ghosts years ago, or thought I had. When I reacquainted with Raoul I did so fresh, with no forbearance of passed transgression on either parties. We were new. I always felt he believed I cheated on him, or that perhaps I was some sort of sex maniac. Now I knew that feeling was accurate. Somehow, though, I would never fully know the truth about those early days. In the end, it was the attention of other boys who drove us apart. Raoul had been caught up in the wave. I always felt rather than cheat on me, he let me go only to find another. The terms of our reuniting were always open, especially because so much time had passed. I had to decide at what cost to my dignity I would suffer for the love of Raoul. Or if I should suffer at all.

"Nick." Raoul couldn't look at me.

"Look, Raoul, just do whatever." I grabbed the bottle on the counter never minding what it was and poured a shot. The label read: "Van Gogh Gin."

"Come on, Matt, let's go." I walked passed Raoul before he could say another thing. We headed towards the door. I could hear Raoul sniffling as we made our exit. "Nick." I heard him call, but did not answer. Finally, as we reached the door, he called once more, "Nick, wait!" He ran over.

"Look, Nick." He grabbed my hand, and looked me in the eye. "Please don't go. I'm sorry, let's just stay here together. Let me get them out of here and I'll explain and…"

I didn't want to see Raoul like this. The tears were beginning to spill from his eyes, and I think it's because he sensed my resolve and the hopelessness of his plight.

"Look, Raoul, there's nothing to talk about. I have nothing else to say."

"Just let me explain," he looked at me and glanced over at Matt.

"If you were going to explain it, you would have already." I pushed passed him and opened the door. Matt was close behind me as we headed out into the dim lit hallway of the Planet Hollywood Hotel.

17

Since the dawn of mankind, there has only been one way for them to subject themselves to perfect peace. The recognition of *we* as a whole. The realizations of the limitless connections we share. There is more to it than the eyes see. Where there may not be a futuristic matrix, a worst-case scenario, there may be another scenario of subtle mind control manipulating to ends we don't know. The means of such pervasive control is seen for the last two to three centuries through religion, governmental and monetary systems, and finally media and propaganda. Stifle the art. The recognition of energy, the depth of meaning behind the concept, has been torn from our paradigm so that we don't see our unity, we don't see ourselves as eternal, we don't see how we share more with everything and everyone than we realize. Perhaps the world view is too limited. What cannot be seen beyond the great blue ceiling is unaccounted. Has history always been this way? Have the masses always been so distracted and confused?

There was a point in my life where I began to take responsibility for my actions and my feelings, and expected the same from others. Raoul, I wouldn't think, would expect any less from me; I sometimes thought that's what he always wanted of me. Anyway, when I began to take account for myself, I found a great peace because I could forgive everyone who'd transgressed me, or anyone I may have been angry at. I began to see a lesson in altercations, and they became less and less and less. I found myself more at peace, more at peace. I found it easy to let the energy flow; I didn't attach myself to things or people as much, though that isn't to say storms didn't brew, because when they did I let them blow over methodically. I felt a storm churning inside me now. What was I to think of Raoul? We'd both been through so much the first time around, was it worth another? True, I was aroused by and flirted with Mattie, but I was bringing him home first, only to find my high school sweetheart a human skewer for two strange men, though one of them looked familiar to me for some reason.

"It was the first time I was going to try something like that with Raoul," I confessed to Mattie as we rode the elevator down to Casino Level. Mattie looked at me sympathetically, his face peering sweet and angelic in its boyish charm. He grabbed my hand.

"Look, it sucks what happened between you and your boyfriend." He moved closer to me. I felt his hips press against mine. "You're with me now. At least for tonight. So, forget about him."

He grabbed my face and pulled me to him. His lips embraced mine tenderly at first, but then passionately. I let him kiss me and soon then returned the kiss. Smooth and plump, his lips were strong against mine, his tongue curious and slick swirling around mine. My hands explored his body, gripping, rubbing, caressing from his shoulders to his ass, his hips. He was warm all over. He gyrated his hips into mine, we both fully aroused, grinded into each other. The casino level sped towards us. What fortunes did I need that I didn't have in this elevator, this transient love lust that found me in a moment of need? Matthew. Mine for the night. We pulled away from our embrace as the bell sounded our arrival to casino level. Our eyes never parted.

"Thank you," I said, a smile creeping from the corners of my mouth. However it had to be, Mattie would serve as the distraction I needed. We exited the elevators, walking passed the grand red-and-white hallways, and the glass windows that revealed the poolside terrace. The closest place to catch a drink was the Halo Bar. I didn't think Fat Tuesday would be appropriate or romantic. I really didn't want to go there. I remembered Neville's party, too, which we'd definitely stop by soon.

We walked through the casino, a bit of vertigo tinging my perception. Latent psilocybin effect turned the striped neon pillars and light fixtures into tiger marks and grinning toothy smiles. Impressions of a Cheshire Cat bounced in my mind. There were people now. Lots of them: talking and chatting and drinking and gambling. There were was a rush from winners on a hot streak. Dealers were calling their hands. The slots were clinging and chiming. Music was pumping. Hip hop beats were pulsating. Lyrics were rapping. Women half dressed in black garments danced and gyrated on miniature platforms and above bars. All of Vegas was awake and out, electric energy flashing through the room and they were all oblivious to the pain and confusion I'd been experiencing; they could all care less who I ended up with. I felt intoxicated, but moved ahead. Mattie was close behind me. We headed straight out, passed the mayhem and the new and pretend money and went into the Halo Bar at the casino entrance. It sat encircled in the middle of the Miracle Mile Mall, the entrance to the PH casino floor lit up with huge neon letters that read: CASINO. At first the curving walls of the Halo Bar were a chilled, neon blue, but they gradually changed colors. The staple light fixture of a jeweled color changing orb hung above the bar. There was a moderate amount of others sitting at the bar and at some of the chairs that lined the inner circumference of the bar. We entered and walked up to the bar sitting on white chairs. I tapped my hands on the bar to the music, bobbed my head. There were screens behind the bar; the giant jeweled orb changed colors as light shimmered on it. The bartender mixed our drinks, and we moseyed over to a table at the corner of the bar wall in front of the casino entrance. We had a view of the slot action, as well as the tourists and sightseers who strolled around shopping, assorted drinks and snacks in their hands.

Mattie sat across from me. His eyes were wide and shined. He seemed to glow. I was glad to have this beautiful boy so interested. I still wasn't sure what to make of our relation. Was this a one-time Vegas fling? He reciprocated—instigated his lust, but was there something deeper to it? He appeared content that Raoul and I had a falling out. I wasn't sure. I kind of wanted to avoid thinking about it. It seemed in this day it was getting harder to find a person of genuine interest. What you were finding were individuals more interested in one-offs, and pragmatists who found someone new every few months. My world view was changing. I was beginning to see the abundance in life, in all aspects. I tried not to think about it too much and just enjoy the ride.

"So what exactly did you order again?" Mattie asked.

I had ordered a stiff gin drink. I was definitely fishing in deeper waters. "Oh, it's called a Hemmingway's Smile. It's mostly gin and lemon juice."

"Oh. That sounds good. Except, I don't think I've tried gin."

"Well there was gin in that Long Island you had earlier."

"Oh."

"Would you like to try it straight up?" There wasn't much to share, as the drink was served in a short, stout, chilled glass. But I didn't mind. There was a cocktail waitress I noticed making rounds.

"Sure." He placed his drink aside, a cherry vodka sour, a standard libation for the uninitiated and typically sober. His eyes crinkled, and lips puckered in a cute way as he sipped at the cup. "Oh, that tingles!"

"I'm sure it does." Mattie was a cute boy. I wanted to know more about him. "So tell me about yourself. You said you're from Texas. You know, my family is from Texas."

"That's cool. Yeah. Born and raised," he nodded.

"You don't have that famous Texas accent."

"Yeah, a lot people say that. Or they look for my horse and cowboy hat." He smiled, rolling his eyes. "I think that's more the people from like, New Mexico or something." I laughed. He did, too. "Although I do say 'ya'll' sometimes." He sipped his drink.

"So when was the last time you went?" he asked.

"Where?" I asked.

"To Texas," he clarified.

"Oh. Well, I used to live there, you know. Before moving west. I still visit my family from time to time, but not much in the last few years."

"So you're an ex-Texan?"

"All my exes live in Texas."

"Oh, god, I love George Strait. He's fine for his age," he blushed a little.

"So you're a two-stepper, huh?" I asked, amused.

"Well, I can never find a dancing partner. Most boys just have no rhythm. Or they can't lead. Can you dance?"

"Maybe I should surprise you sometime."

Mattie smiled again, his eyes sparkled and I warmed up. I finished my Hemmingway drink. Mattie took another sip of his cherry vodka sour and asked, "Where did you live in Texas?"

"Well, I was born in San Antonio and I lived in Austin for a while. I really enjoyed Austin. San Antonio was quaint, but I had small pond syndrome and had to get out. I used to like going down to the beach, too. I went once during the winter and it was hot as heck. I met with a friend and we went down to Mexico. In fact, it was Neville. The dude hosting the party we're gonna check out."

"Cool. I've never been to Mexico."

"Well, I've heard so many different horror stories about the place," Mattie nodded at this statement, his eyes wide as he sipped his cherry vodka sour. I continued, "But I didn't find it all that disturbing. I think it's more a border town fear. Don't go to the border, you'll get shot; you'll get decapitated by drug cartels; you'll get diarrhea if you drink the water; you'll get raped if you're a woman. It goes on and on. But none of that happened to me. Then again, we went pretty far into Mexico. Southwest of Mexico City."

"That sounds awesome. Have you been to Europe?"

"No, not yet. But that is coming up on my checklist." I smiled at him. He sipped his drink. The waitress came by. I ordered a Hurricane. All this talk about Mexico gave me a craving for something tropical.

"So have you hung out at the PH before?" I asked Mattie.

"No, this is my first time here." He looked around, never putting down his cherry vodka sour. "It's kinda funny we're in a mall." People were walking around us, looking at us like voyeurs behind sunglasses and ice cream cones. My Hurricane arrived. A ruckus from the casino pulled our attention. Beneath the glaring, neon "CASINO" entrance sign, just beyond the threshold, a pair of young rabble rousers were striking it rich on the slot machines. They whooped and jumped up and down. My Hurricane was delicious. I could taste the deep rums mixed just right with the fresh juices.

"Yeah. It really is a pretty cool casino. The suites are amazing. I wish you could have seen more of mine, but Neville's is pretty awesome, too."

"I'll take any suite we can have some privacy together." He said nonchalantly, a devilish grin curling up at the corner of his lip. I took a heavy pull at my drink.

"Would you like to try? I think you'll really like this." I let Mattie sip from my straw. His eyes locked on mine as he pulled and pulled and pulled.

"That is so refreshing! Where did you learn all these drinks?"

"Ah, you live, you learn, as Alanis Morrissette once said."

"Who?"

I had to laugh inside. I didn't know why I made an Alanis Morrisette reference; I hadn't listened to the old bag in over a decade at the height of my adolescence, before I turned to heavier and darker things. I guess I figured the younger gays might have known. Or I just felt like being a dork. Oh, how wrong I was to have assumed. What an ass.

"Oh, nobody." I shook my head, this time I being the one who blushed. "Just somebody who was cool for a short period of time in the mid 1990s." Even that period of time had now begun to seem distant. But what was still more appalling to me was calling anything 90s retro. 90s were not retro. The 80s were retro. The 90s had yet to be labeled. Like the 50s were the oldies. The 60s were the classics. The 70s were funky. Everyone has had a problem with the 2000s and after. The 10s? It just doesn't feel right. The Hurricane vanished much quicker than I had expected.

"Do you have a boyfriend back in Texas, Mattie?" I asked, and Mattie suddenly looked very demur.

"Well, no." My heart dropped for him. "I'm not really out back home. So nobody knows."

"Well, as long as you know what you want, when you're ready, you'll be able to come out."

I could feel Mattie's foot rubbing up against mine and up and down my ankle and up the side of my shin.

"I know I want you," he said.

"Shall we to the party, my good man?" I asked, giving Mattie a wink. The drinks were beginning to take effect on me again. I could feel them slowly swooning in, unlike before, as the white wore off. I was slightly taken aback by the resounding clarity I had though. I wasn't tired. I wasn't wired. But I was still very aware of everything. Like I was aware of how drunk I was becoming, but somehow had just enough control not to go over the edge.

"Yeah, I think that'd be fun."

The waitress came by, I asked for the check which she

delivered without leaving, and before she could walk off I gave her a couple bills and bid her a good evening. Mattie and I got up, both feeling randy and ready to see what sweet desserts my friend Neville and his wife Gladys had in store for us.

Part

~

Three

18

We arrived at Neville's suite, which like ours, was at the end of a long, dimly lit hallway of regular guest rooms. The entrance, two intimidating black doors equipped with twin, stainless steel knockers loomed before us. The door knockers seemed heavy. I lift the thick silver knob and gave it a gruff rap. The knocker was indeed heavy. We waited. Mattie was behind me. Suddenly I felt a pair of arms reach around me and hug at my waist. I felt a strong chin rest on my shoulder. I leaned my head back until I nuzzled his head. I felt comfortable. I raised the knocker again and rapped twice more. Finally I heard a lock clicking and as the door cracked open an immense sound boomed from behind the door. The bass alone sent vibrations into a tizzy out in the hallway. I could feel my skin prickle. Mattie and I stood straight as the door opened. A strange, tall man stood at the door. I didn't know who he was. He wore dark clothes. He was pale with a modest five o' clock shadow. He seemed somewhat brooding.

"Come on in," he said. "The water's fine." A sudden, silly grin wrenched his lips. His pupils were miniscule. He twitched and wiped his nose. He was wired. *This must be a drug guy*, I thought. We entered the suite. The beats of the bass pounded in my chest. I couldn't tell if the table in the anteroom vibrated or if my eyes were bouncing in their sockets. Visions of Bruce Willis in his *Die Hard* days plastered the wall. As we walked forward, my eyes were pulled to the center of the room by an expansive panoramic window with a miraculous view of Las Vegas Boulevard. The melee of beauty and grandeur: the Bellagio Fountains dancing and lit, frolicking and swaying to an unheard hymn; the Paris Hotel dominant before the mock Eiffel Tower that glittered, elegant against the passing lights of traffic and traffic lights. People sat here and there along this grand, lengthy couch. There was plenty of seating. As we entered the room, my eyes were drawn to my left, where a Jacuzzi sat in the middle of the living room. Behind it was the bathroom, which you could see straight through to from over the Jacuzzi. Against the backdrop of the music, there was a welcoming socialness in the room I didn't recognize at first. People were having fun. People I'd never seen before. I wondered where Neville had found all these people. And I wondered where Neville was. We walked further in where I ran into another piece of Bruce Willis paraphernalia, a costume from some movie he'd made. Too funny. There was a table where some people sat that gave another spectacular view of the fountains and the Eiffel Tower. Immediately across from the table was a nice modern bar where I found Neville, mixing drinks.

"Hey, guys!" He kind of did a double take when he noticed Mattie was not Raoul. "Guy."

"Neville, good to see you!" I reached over and gave him a hug. "It feels like it's been forever!"

"Yeah, tell me about it, *guay*, standing us up for happy hour and all."

"Yeah, it's been one of those nights, man."

Neville was looking over my shoulder at Mattie. "This is Mattie from Austin, Texas." I introduced the two and Mattie reached forward and shook Neville's hand.

"Thanks for the party."

"Hey, no prob! I love Texas! I used to live there, but Cali was my first home when I got to the states! Nice people in Texas."

"Well, not everybody thinks so."

"Well, that's true. People from New York hate you guys for some reason. But the French love you, so it can't be half bad!" We laughed. "What're y'all having to drink? I'll mix it up right here! Bam!"

"Oh, awesome." I exclaimed. "You're suite is frickin' awesome!"

"I know, man." Neville clamped his heavy hand on my shoulder and shook. "I told you someday I'd be *muy chingon!*"

Mattie laughed. In fact, he snorted. We both looked at him smiling. I guess he'd heard the term before.

"Well, Neville-san, I think I'll have a good old fashioned margarita."

"Patron?"

"What else?"

"Yessir! Coming right up! And how about this fine, young man? What'll it be?"

Mattie looked at me. "Oh, I'll have the same." He smiled.

"Two Top O' the Pops Margaritas coming right up!" Neville started to pour and mix. In seconds he was done.

"Damn, Neville, where'd you learn to mix like that?"

"You forget I worked at a restaurant and bar for about a decade."

"Oh, yeah. You weren't always *muy chingon.*" We laughed again.

"So, what's going on? Where's Raoul?" I felt my muscles tense up. I took Neville's margarita and downed it in two seconds flat.

"He was busy. Can I have another?"

"Sure, buddy. Anything for you."

Neville mixed another margarita and then Mattie and I wandered back into the living room, walking up to the window, drink in hand.

"That's an amazing view," Mattie remarked. "This is an

amazing suite."

"I know," I agreed, turning and looking around. "I'm surprised no one's in the Jacuzzi."

"Maybe we could."

"Hmm, I don't know. I already took a shower." Mattie turned to me; his eyes were serious and twisted with the slightest of seduction. "But we're gonna need to get clean, after we get dirty." He moved close to me and leaned in. We looked out the window. The fountains were dancing again.

"Why don't you and me find some place to be alone?" I asked him, finally getting up the courage to take him. He turned at me and smiled. "I've been waiting all night."

We walked in front of the leather sofa, barely noticed by the group of individuals drinking, smoking, and lounging around. They were gabbing amongst each other, oblivious to our presence. But I got an eyeful. They were a mixed crowd. Some seemed young, most about mine and Neville's age. Some of the people looked familiar, like celebrities you don't recognize in person, but I thought otherwise of it. Mattie and I walked on; there was another table and the panoramic view continued, revealing the Paris hotel, its majesty lit with a veneer of sophistication. We walked down a hall. I'd tug at my margarita here and there. Finally we came to a door that led to another bedroom. The room was modern and chic, the black and white motif had continued into this room. There were red accents here and there, like the lamps and some throw pillows. The bed looked plush and comfortable, and matched the rooms color coordination. The instant the door closed Mattie was on me, kissing me. I grabbed his face, my palms cupping his cheeks. My lips reached for his, embraced them. Our tongues flirted playfully; I tasted him, and instantly longed for a deeper taste. My hands moved down his body, caressed the length of his back. I grasped the swollen curves of his buttocks firmly and thrust my pelvis into his. He moaned even as I kissed him. We became a mix of extremities removing clothes and caressing torsos, arms, thighs. Finally he pushed me away and pushed me to the bed. I was astounded. He was much more aggressive than I had expected. He reached for my pants and unbuttoned them, releasing my cock; it had long ached to be free, and now bulged before him. Mattie instantly went down on me, the warmth of his mouth at first sending shockwaves through my body. I laid back for a moment, hardly believing he was new to this practice. I let him continue for a time, caressing his soft, strawberry blond hair. I was feeling the drink; I was feeling the warm, wet tickling and sucking; it was all becoming too much. I felt my body seize up, and almost as if he had sensed it, Mattie stopped. He unbuckled his pants and moved up my body. He was a beautiful young man, indeed. His body was strong and full, but lean and firm. He had a beautiful cock that jutted thickly from a patch of thick, straight hair. I moved him toward me, my hands on his thighs, massaging his muscles all the way to his ass. I moved him forward so that his body was over me, straddling me at my neck. I fellated him tenderly at first, as he moaned loudly. He tasted a bit salty. I stroked the smoothness of the soft skin and exposed head with my tongue. I licked up his dribble of pre-cum. The motion quickened and he began to thrust his pelvis into my mouth. I sucked deeply allowing the length of his penis to the back of my throat. I moved my tongue along the shaft to the scrotum. His entire body seemed to seizure as I licked and fondled each teste. I continued in this fashion, until eventually, I had moved behind him, my tongue guiding the way. He tasted good all over. I was ready to enter him. When he felt this, he stopped and turned.

"Do you have protection?" He asked.

"Well, no, I don't think I do." I didn't know what else to say.

"Well…" He trailed off in thought. He turned back to me, our bodies against each other. "Well, I'm clean. Are you?"

"I tested negative before I got with Raoul again. I haven't

had any problems since. And we were safe anyway. He insisted on it."

I felt Mattie's energy relent and then release. He leaned towards me, his buttocks warm against my stomach and hips, and we kissed again. I felt my mind melt into his as our flesh connected; our lips told the tale without words of the deep longing inside, with the call of the void that longed to be filled, even if for a minute, with the warmth of acceptance, the love that belonged to all, but was forgotten to the ferocious darts of apathy and survivalism, individualism. These *isms* could mix themselves into a foray of unnecessariness; that is why they were created to begin with, but I longed to feel the slippery, soft flesh of this young lover melt into my mouth like the most decadent chocolate. It was then in that heat of passion where we more than kissed, but connected, that I entered him in a gesture that glided warmly into a path accepting and familiar. Mattie winced and hummed in pleasure. I pushed until I was deep in him, the heat of his body like a hearth. I felt the electricity of our oneness unlike any before. Any before may have been a run through the emotions, but my soul opened, and I felt it flow away from me, I felt it dance and swirl with Mattie's, even oblivious to the dynamic mesh of colors and sparking rainbows. What love that could be felt by all, there was no extent to ridicule, just list; even as I panted in deep concentration, there was no need. We found a rhythm that complimented each other as I moved in and out, engorged by the warmth of his being. He gyrated his hips, grinding into me, taking me deeper. Our flesh moistened with perspiration. Beads of sweat rolled down my temples, dripped to his shoulders. The taking of this firm and giving vessel had brought me to a home that consoled my very existence until I erupted no finer a truth than that which my creator had intended. The love of my rupture, as my body spasmed into his and he gripped me tightly at that moment of orgasm, burst into magnificent kaleidoscopes of life that would never see the day of existence shared into Mattie as I dripped with perspiration and moistened his skin and laid into him, and he embraced me and held me close and closed his eyes and dreamed within the briefest of instances of eternity in the arms of a lover who would never part. It was in the parting of that instant the recognition of departure came, for the fleeting pleasure would subside even as I held his body close, even as he deigned to release me, even as he held me inside him and clutched the memory of my existence, even as my eyelids became heavy and for a moment heavenly paradise sparkled before my eyes, comforted, my body close to his. I knew this feeling would not last. I held on to it as long as I could. I listened to the innocent bells of childhood. I longed for the youth that had led me down these paths of discovery. As I held Mattie's body close, I briefly thought about how I came to this place. My past with Raoul flashed through my mind. Our love. Our separation. Our reunion. Life had become an unsolvable puzzle after I first left Raoul. It had become a nightmare of self-discernment and introspection; I did not understand self-control; I only wished to placate my misery with drunkenness and other distortive minions. I didn't understand who I was. I had become some sort of monster. I had become reactive. I was locked into the flight or fight mode. I was ignorant. But, now with this beautiful boy lying close to me, I gave no more room for those thoughts to breathe. I only wanted to slip deep inside Mattie, not just into his body as I did then, but into his soul. I wanted to meld into him, to become part of him. He turned over, I slid out of him. He looked me in the eyes. I felt as if he'd been listening to my entire private conversation—as if he'd been in my head the whole time, and he kissed me. It was then that we made love. We did not reveal the tendencies of lust; that was now behind us; now our souls connected, even as our eyes closed and we fell into each other, dependent upon each other's' very breath to live, to thrive if only for an instant. We melted into the golden hues and deepened shadows cast by the Vegas lights outside our window.

At some point in the night Mattie and I left the room we'd shared ourselves in. I felt close to him. I almost ached at the thought of his departure when this night was over. I didn't want to seem creepy or desperate to him, but I had grown fond of him. I couldn't fathom a long distance relationship, and so the idea of separation hung in the knowing. I didn't want to let on to Mattie, but I was sure he could feel it either way.

We emerged back into the living room. The music still buzzed and bumped mercilessly, but was tastefully written with a certain amount of artisanship that was not common among this day's promoted, Top 40 musicians. I grooved into it as we walked past the panoramic Las Vegas Boulevard view to the star bar of black-and-white design, where Neville had previously served up tenaciously deft margaritas. I held Mattie's hand as we crossed over.

We reached the bar to find Neville still present mixing some sort of martini. He looked at us with a slight shock, almost like when we first came in. Neville was never good at hiding his bewilderment.

"Hey, guys! What's up?" He looked at me, but not in the eyes. Instead his eyes dodged back and forth nervously as if distracted. I wasn't sure what to think, but then again I was fairly drunk.

"I don't know. What's up with you?" I asked. I didn't know what else to say. "Well, what's up with you? Enjoying the party?"

"Yeah, man. Not much going on here." He gave a fake chuckle, "I've just been mixing drinks. I don't even know what Gladys is up to." He looked around real quick. "I thought you guys left or something. Where you been? A lot of crazy shit's going on around here."

"What did you expect? This is Bruce Willis' suite. Some

crazy shit is bound to happen here."

"You think he's been here?"

"I don't know, but probably." I squeezed Mattie's hand just so he'd know I still remembered he was there, and I pulled it forward and kissed it. Neville looked at me funnily and kind leaned back, his eyes widened. He looked down. I flinched, not knowing what to say.

"Tell you what, Neville. How about we go find Gladys and then we'll blow this party and grab a bite to eat." Neville looked at me wide eyed. He looked vacant as he pondered my proposition, and then responded, "Well, I mean I don't want to leave my suite alone, but I'm down. Go find her ass, it's somewhere around here. I am tired of making drinks like a good goddamn little hostess!"

"That's right!" Mattie and I walked on passed the bar to the bedroom at the back of the suite. I hadn't seen here among the assemblage of partygoers, so I figured if any place, that's where she'd be. The door was closed; I opened the door slowly at first. As we entered the master suite I saw Gladys sitting on the bed at the center of a group of individuals all leaning, lying, or sitting on the bed beside her. Raoul was there. Gladys was holding a glass pipe in her hand; Raoul was torching it as she rolled it back and forth. The glass pipe became opaque with white smoke after a few moments, and she inhaled. I knew exactly what they were doing, and it dawned on me then that this was most likely the substance Raoul had me snorting before I left for Bond. I was surprised at the extent of Raoul's usage. The group was fixated on the pipe and torch, and didn't seem to notice us until we walked further into the room.

"Oh, hey, Nick!" Gladys greeted. "Hey, would you mind closing that door?" I reached back and closed it. Mattie looked at me disconcertedly.

"Did you wanna stay?" I asked Mattie.

'Well, I mean..." his voice trailed off. I knew he didn't want to. I began to feel terrible.

"You guys aren't gonna go are you?" Raoul called. Envy trailed in his voice. A chill ran up my spine. I paused. I felt a thunder on the horizon of my mind; the wind began to pick up. To be honest I hadn't thought of what I was going to do when next I saw Raoul. I didn't want to make a big scene of anything. I had to think about Mattie.

"You know what? I think we need to get a drink first." I turned to Mattie. "Shall we?" We turned and walked out. I looked back. Raoul sat with a disappointed look on his face. Gladys was toking back a fine white cloud. "I'll get the door."

Mattie and I walked back to the bar, charmed as ever by its mod black-and-white design. Neville looked like he'd been sweating.

"So, what's going on? Did you find Gladys?" Neville was still mixing drinks.

"Oh, yeah. She's tied up at the moment."

"Raoul was there, too?" This seemed more like a statement than a question.

"Oh, you knew?"

"Huh? What?" More fake chuckles and a wave of the hand and a shake of the head, "Of course not, buddy! You know I would have told you if I knew!" Neville chuckled nervously, his cover blown.

"Well, that's fine," I said definitively. "They are smoking out. Mattie and I wanted to get some drinks. I'll make them." I walked behind the bar. The music continued to pump in the background. It seems someone had turned the music down a notch, or I was swollen headed.

"What on earth are you playing, man? It sounds awesome!"

"Oh, just a DJ friend of mine I found! He's spinning it pretty hot, huh?"

"Yeah! I haven't been to party with music this good since I threw one myself half a decade ago! You're learning."

"These parties only come so often, man! May as well make it top notch."

I put together a quick concoction. The bar had everything I could need. I mixed a touch of grenadine, two shots of Jack, some cola, served it on the rocks and put a cherry on top. That was for Mattie. I would require something stronger. I didn't want wood grain alcohols, though. No trashcan punch for me. I had lost count of how many times I'd let this demon out of the bottle. I grabbed the Tanqueray Gin and mixed in a spritz of carbonated water with three shots served on the rocks; this could very well have been my undoing, but this was the last night in Vegas; I could look beyond that.

"Nice mix," Neville remarked. I handed Mattie his drink. He lit up. "Jack and cherry Coke for my darling."

He sipped. Gently his eyes lit up. "This tastes great!"

I took a pull at my drink. The immediate spice of the gin flared my glands. I imbibed.

"So did you still wanna grab a bite to eat? I could order room service," Neville suggested.

"Well, I kind of feel like stepping out for a bit." I smiled. "This is our last night in Vegas, man! Why don't you join us? Gladys is here, I'm sure she and Raoul can manage without us! They'll hold it down. Besides I'm pretty sure they'll be wired enough to handle anything that comes up."

"Alright, cool." He poured a shot of Patron and downed it in one motion. He sighed, satisfied. "You'll never guess what, buddy." He reached into his pocket and pulled out a pair of keys, "I bought me some motorcycles." He laughed with pleasure. I took another pull of my drink.

"That's pretty crazy, man! I know you always said you wanted one."

"And you, too!"

"Well, yeah, but I haven't gotten a bike or anything, yet" I laughed.

"Well, I'll give you one, man."

I was taken aback, "What? I couldn't accept something like that!"

"Well, why not, man? You've always been there for me. I don't see why I can't just give you a bike?"

I was out of words. My head already began to spin a bit from the gin, and the tequila, and the music. It had gotten funky and light, a strong beat fixated on making you dance. Some of the people in the room were doing just that. They swayed back and forth. Two women couple danced merrily bouncing and spinning. I had enjoyed my experience in Vegas despite everything that had happened. These instances had all become learning curves for me, and I could only be grateful for those who chose to stand by me.

"Well, I guess we can go check them out."

Each of us took another drink, Neville pouring himself another shot of the top shelf, silver tequila.

"No rush, guys, we can always take our drinks with us. We're in Vegas, remember?" We laughed and moved towards the door. That funny man that had opened the door when we first arrived was still standing by the door.

"I see you probably met Patrick. He's our door man." Patrick smiled at us. He opened the door for us. On the other side of the door was a young man who was coming in. I immediately recognized him as one of the two I had caught with Raoul. He wore a Daft Punk T-shirt from their *Discovery* album era. Suddenly I remembered why he was the one that was vaguely familiar, and I finally placed his face. He hadn't had a shirt on when I busted the three getting it on in our suite, but I had seen him earlier at the Luxor. He was the guy washing his hands next to Raoul in the bathroom. I recalled Raoul fastening his belt and adjusting his pants as he exited. My imagination quickly soared and my heart sank. The guy had also tensed up sensing some sort of current between us, and suddenly as the charge surged, a flash of electricity struck me and I saw my fists moving faster than they've ever moved before. I pummeled him. The commotion was sudden, the outburst so random it startled everyone once they realized an altercation was taking place beneath the pulsing bass and driving rhythm. I remembered shouts of "Oh, my god!" and "Are they for real?" "Are they fighting?"

Neville moved to get right in the middle of it. Patrick the doorman did as well. I only wanted to make sure that if Raoul was gonna be kissing this guy tonight that'd he'd have something to think of me by. There was blood. Mattie was jumping up and down; he had backed away the moment I fell into motion. I walked out of the room, stepping over this asshole and down the hall. I hadn't suffered any harm. Neville and Mattie followed behind me. They were stunned. I had sudden tunnel vision. I didn't even feel like I was thinking.

"Oh, my god, Nick, you just clobbered that guy!" Mattie shouted.

"He deserved it," I huffed as I moved quickly down the dim lit hallways. Rows of doors flew passed me.

"But, who was he?" Mattie asked, "That wasn't one of the guys from earlier, was it?"

"Yeah, man that was pretty fierce. What the hell?" Neville chimed in.

"Sorry, guys, I'm not typically prone to violence, but I thought it best I not keep my feelings bottled up." I walked on, feeling the clouds subside. They followed.

*   *   *

This was now. We stood in the lobby of the hotel which was at the back of the building. Everything lit up in mod colors and shapes, all LED or fluorescent from the walls, to pillars, to the fixtures behind the check in desk, the crystalline spherical chandeliers. The lobby itself was dimly lit. Neville had called down and asked to have the bikes prepped. We waited maybe two or three minutes before a pair of dark motorcycles pulled up. Neville's face lit up.

"Let's check them out," he said, whacking my chest with the back of his hand and walking forward. He thanked and tipped the attendant, who walked off happily.

I looked at the bikes; they were twin Harleys, Sportster Forty-Eights. I had never ridden before. I was beginning to feel the shock. Mattie stood close by me.

"Well, whatdoya think, buddy?" Neville trembled with excitement.

"Holy fucking Christ, Neville! I don't know what to say? Is this real, or am I drunk?"

"Both, ya jerk!" Neville laughed.

I turned to Mattie. The night time air flowed deep into my lungs, polluted only slightly by the exhaust of cars and limos pulling in and out of the hotel driveway. Mattie only smiled.

"So are we gonna go riding, or what?"

"I thought you just pulled them down to look at them," I said, woozing a bit. "Well, I don't know that I should handle a machine at this time. Is it still drinking and driving if you're on a bike?" I hesitated, then conceded, "Ah, hell, why not give it a chance."

"All right, now you're talking! Now looks who's *chingon*!"

A sudden commotion came from behind us. It rippled from inside, in the lobby, like spiking energy. I felt it prickle the back of my neck even as the upset voices registered and I turned around. Raoul was pushing through people, already out the door. He was half-running, jumping, and dodging around the guests and tourists.

"Nicholas! Nicholas! How could you!" He was yelling like I'd never heard him yell before. I never knew his voice could sound off with such animosity. I looked at him, considering a clean get away from the oncoming madness. The boy was wired out his mind. I knew it instantly as flashes of Gladys and him hovering around that glass pipe and that white smoke flooded my mind.

"Maybe we *should* go."

"Oh, my god, this is crazy!"

"Look, man, I don't know what's going on, but you two just take off, and I'll talk to Raoul and try to calm him down."

"You're a true friend, but that is not Raoul you're dealing with. Mattie," I turned to the boy who had paled a bit, but who, at the same time had a strange anticipation in his eyes. "Come on, hop on."

We both straddled the bike. I hit the ignition, revved the motor just as Raoul arrived. Neville instantly wrapped his bulbous arms around Raoul's thin waist, catching him in mid-pounce, as the Harley roared to life. I saw flashes and lights pointing at us, briefly wondered what it was all about and pushed the throttle. Mattie held me closely, tight to my body. I couldn't look back to see what was going on, but I heard more screaming; I heard Raoul yelling at the top of his lungs again. It was a sound I tried to drown out with the roar of the bike.

We pulled onto Harmon Avenue and headed toward the Strip. We'd take a night time ride downtown Las Vegas style, buzzed or not, but long enough to allow Raoul to calm. I'd be headed west soon anyway, back home, and I'd have to pick up all the pieces there. This vacation, as it were, had only provided more personal work, but at the same time, with much gratitude, I recognized that the events that took place only brought to light truths that needed to be seen for my own good, and perhaps for the greater good of us all.

We idled in traffic at a red light waiting to turn on to Las Vegas Boulevard. I heard a horn honk, and the sound of another engine. The light was still red, but it seemed the engine was getting closer. More horns honked. I turned around. Mattie still clung to me. Another motorcyclist approached on a bike, riding between the cars. The pit of my stomach tightened when I realized it was Raoul.

"Shit," I muttered. How'd he get the bike? What happened to Neville? "Mattie, hold tight."

Raoul approached and wasted no time throwing his fists at the both of us. Mattie yelled at Raoul, as did I, but I tried to focus on the road. I revved the engine and hit the throttle, moving forward and around a car that idled at the stop light. We moved onto the sidewalk where a few people had stopped because of the sudden commotion. The people screamed as the bike blazed forward along the side of the casino and resort. The pedestrians were conscious enough to move out the way, realizing we'd use the sidewalk as our escape route. And we did. We sped forward on the sidewalk and popped around the corner as the light turned green. I swerved onto Las Vegas Boulevard, fortunate there was no contending traffic. We rushed down the street, but Raoul was not far behind. The rush of air and lights hit me as we moved. The wind rushed through me, the engine jeered beneath me. Traffic, there was traffic all around. I weaved between cars as the new, majestic recreations of our time—the casinos and hotels, the lights and signs, the shops, bars and restaurants—lit up like 365 days of Christmas stood tall around us and blurred to my peripherals. Looking down the road I could see a wave of green lights. I hit the throttle moving just over the speed limit. I didn't know how far Raoul was behind me. My mind was racing fast as the bike. I ignored the blare of horns as we dodged in and out of traffic; lights and people streamed by. We'd passed up the neon mod spotted façade of the Planet Hollywood, with its Miracle Mile Mall and Cabo Wabo eatery. The Cosmopolitan, the Paris Hotel, the Paris Balloon rose high above the cars and people, as did the Eiffel Tower, and all of these too were momentary visions. I had to focus on protecting Mattie. Speeding drunk on a motorcycle in a busy city like Las Vegas didn't help my case much. Still, we sped on as the lights were green passed the Bellagio. The fountains were noticeably dark, the lake eerily lit so pedestrians might watch their step. A sweltering of people gathered at Mon Ami Gabi, the French restaurant in front of the Paris, unaware of the chase taking place. My heart stopped as the traffic began to back up in front of Balley's. I risked stopping, hoping Raoul had not followed, but within minutes another engine roared. It seemed déjà vu as cars began to honk and the engine progressed toward us.

"Nick, what are we gonna do? I think he's still following us!" Mattie half yelled in my ear.

"I don't know. I'll try to lose him!"

I peeled out from behind the party limo in front of us just as Raoul reached us. We raced between the lanes of cars where people shouted and honked, startled by our behavior. Our Harleys roared as we mowed through the crosswalk and on through the intersection as the light turned green and I barely clipped a passing car.

"Oh my God!" Mattie cried as we moved forward. I had no idea how we'd lose Raoul. What would he do anyway if he caught us? Would it be better to stop this and just duke it out man to man? I contemplated what to do as we road passed Caesar's Palace and its fountains, and the old, classic-looking Serendipity 3 restaurant and the Flamingo Hotel. Traffic cleared a bit, but not for long, and I found myself moving between lanes, though seamless, to pass along quicker and clear more distance from Raoul. As we moved passed Harrah's I saw the flames of the Mirage volcano begin to dance.

"Nick!" I heard a disembodied voice, haggard and blown. "Nick! You get off that bike right now!"

It was Raoul, he'd caught up to us. He began striking his fist at Mattie, and striking me in the shoulder. Cars began to honk at us. I tried to focus on the road, but Raoul's present threat was distracting. I turned in time to see Mattie straighten and strike Raoul in the face. Raoul veered to the right. I hit the throttle and blasted forward. I heard a bloodcurdling scream!

"Oh, shit!" Mattie screamed. "He's still chasing us! And he's coming fast!"

"God! And that's why you never wanna get mixed with a crack addict." I was glad Mattie could not hear me beneath the rush of the wind.

I drove fast in front of the Mirage where the flames of the volcano began to burst and to dance. A crowd had already begun to form along the gates. I made a hard left into the entrance of the hotel, barely missing oncoming traffic. I hoped Raoul would not follow. The light had just turned red, and I heard a commotion of horns and screaming and swearing as I drove full speed into the semicircular entrance of the Mirage Hotel. The volcano display began to really get underway, casting an orange luminance across the resort, causing the Beatles *Love* banner to smolder in an unearthly glow. There were lines of cars leading up to the hotel, and people walking to the entrance all looking at us as we pressed full speed on our black motorcycles. They screamed and winced, running out of the way, jumping off the crosswalks or back into their limos and taxi cabs. Finally we'd made our grand exit as the flames of the volcano began to burst, even from the very lake itself. You could feel the heat as the fire torched the atmosphere.

"Nick!" Raoul yelled behind us.

I flew into oncoming traffic, exiting the Mirage drive-in, taking faith I'd make it, pulling back north onto Las Vegas Boulevard. It was a knee-jerk reaction that caused me to jump the bike over the median in front of Casino Royale, as traffic had backed up due to the red light up ahead. My heart raced; the Harley roared as we soared over the median and drove headfirst into traffic. We shot straight to the sidewalk back on the Mirage side of the boulevard where the volcano display neared its peak, and music and drums were pounding. But the crowd of people paid no attention; they had been watching us since we shot out of the exit, and scattered as we moved toward them. Raoul was behind us still, and had mimicked all the feats we'd performed, except as I took a hard right on the side walk and turned, missing the gated lake, Raoul drove forward, popping a wheelie straight into the manmade pond that circled the Mirage Volcano. People screamed as the Harley crashed into the water, and the volcano released a deft and final ball of flame. I stopped for a moment, looking to see what had become of Raoul, to see if he would surface. The seconds ticked on deepening into hours inside my mind, but eventually I heard a commotion splashing in the water. I could see Raoul kicking and screaming. The show had ended and people had gathered to watch the spectacle. "Drunken man runs Harley into Mirage Lake." I heard sirens in the distance.

"I think we should go Mattie."

"Yeah, me too." He gripped me tight as we kicked off, leaving the excited frenzy behind us.

*   *   *

We rode on. Mattie still held tight. I enjoyed him near me. We moved north on the Strip, the Harley riding smoothly, the purr of the engine warming my seat. The new hotels tapered off to the older relic types that no one seemed to want to visit anymore. They were inexpensive, offered a great value to those who simply wanted to try Vegas out and not do the whole shebang. They were sometime a bit more run down, but by south Strip standards. You probably couldn't find a hotel and casino as nice and replete with history as those you found in Vegas. That was only one reason I knew Vegas and I weren't through, not by a long shot. But, again the thought of returning home; the thought of again having to confront Raoul, and not that I avoided confrontation—I'd much rather resolve than avoid. There was also the thought of parting with Mattie, and that did cause my heart to feel a longing. The boulevard had become surprisingly empty, as the Stratosphere Tower grew before us, a sentinel on the landscape. The crisp Nevada air swirled around us. We stopped at a light on Sahara, where the now-closed hotel and casino of the same name stood behind construction walls. This hotel, too, would soon be revamped and re-opened. The construction of the north end Strip had been gradual. I didn't know what had become of Raoul or where he'd gone, but I was glad he was away from us. The light turned green and we rode forward, the desert wind prickling, a constant companion, as we drove up Las Vegas Boulevard.

19

We'd ridden all the way down the Boulevard until we were downtown. I didn't feel like going back to the PH, though I did want to contact Neville to make sure he was fine. I asked Mattie if he'd mind if I checked into a hotel down on Fremont, just to get away from all the madness. Everything would resolve itself in time, I figured. Mattie said he'd stay the night with me. We rode the bike into the D Hotel. On the way to the lobby, I booked a room on my cell phone so all we had to do was walk up to the counter, verify our identities, and get the room key.

In the room I called Neville, and Mattie called his parents. He was letting them know that he was okay and that he was with a friend. The story with Neville was not as simple. Neville reported that after we'd zoomed off on the Harley he continued to struggle with Raoul, until finally Raoul broke free and knocked him over. Neville, being naturally clumsy already, fell into oncoming traffic and was hit by one of Gladys' favorite cars, a Mazda Miata. Albeit the car was traveling at fifteen miles an hour, the weight of his thick body cracked the windshield and he fell through. That's when Raoul hopped on the second Harley and began to chase us. Unfortunately for him, his troubles had only just begun. Already wired off huge amounts of adrenaline and liquor, Neville was able to get out of the car. He momentarily thought of taking chase, but that was when he was jumped by two security guards who tackled him to the ground.

A mess with bits of glass adhered to him by blood and sweat, Neville went down hard and fast. They took him inside the hotel, quick to return their drive-in and lobby area to a state of normalcy.

Neville strived to maintain some resemblance of composure and dignity, even while cuffed in plastic arm ties, but insisted that he was an esteemed guest of this hotel in a high level suite, and he demanded justice because his bike had just been stolen. Unfortunately for him the security guards only saw Neville and Raoul struggling and had assumed that Neville was trying to jack Raoul's bike.

Once the mess had been cleared, and Neville had proved his ownership of the Harley, he filed a police report, refused an ambulance or any type of medical care, and left his contact info for the owner of the car whose windshield he had fallen through. He went back to his suite where he found Gladys running lines of coke on the table in front of the couches and the grand view of Las Vegas, which even now was lit and dazzling. People stood around her, some smoking, some drinking, some doing a combination of the two. The music continued to play. But Neville had had enough, and now he needed to be the one soaking in the Jacuzzi. He pulled the plug on the speakers, sinking the room into an absolute silence. People stopped talking awkwardly in mid-sentence. He flipped the lights on. Gladys looked up.

"All right, guys, I know it's early, but party's over. I just fell through a window. You can take some favors if you want, but I need some alone time. Now."

Everyone seemed to deflate a little bit. There was a rush of sighs and "awws," but really, they were in Vegas, there were thousands of places the night could take them. So he rushed them out just a bit. Gladys, who initially poised to strike Neville for ending the party, relented and offered him a line.

"Here you go, baby, this will take away the pain." The line was a foot long, but Neville moved up the table like a pro.

"So, you're gonna stay at the D tonight?" Neville asked.

"Yeah, we're already down here. And we had a hell of a chase. I'll tell you about it tomorrow."

"What about Raoul?"

"I don't know, to be honest. I kind of don't want to think about it right now."

"That's cool, man. Well, give us a call tomorrow and maybe we can do breakfast or lunch or something."

"We'll do brunch." I ended our call and turned to Mattie. He was stretched out on the bed. I moved over to him and put my arm across his chest.

"I'm sorry for everything that happened today."

He turned to me and smiled, "Don't be sorry. It was actually a very good evening." He pecked me on my nose quickly.

"My parents were just kind of freaked out because apparently there was some sort of gun shooting that happened at the Excalibur. I told them they needed to get out of their suite and do something instead of watching television." He laughed, and I did too, but only because I'd been at the shooting and was surprised its news finally made its way around.

"It's been a pretty crazy night, hasn't it?" I looked him deep in the eyes and we kissed again. I moved his body closer. We breathed into each other. We made love again. This time a gentler love, an everlasting love of tense and fragile bodies entwining momentarily, and when we'd finished we lay in spoons, cuddled close together, warm and comfortable with each other. We fell asleep, oblivious to the booming noises and concerts of the street below, and I slept a deep and satisfying sleep, my heart content as it had never been in my life. When I woke in the morning, Mattie was gone. There was note written on a hotel notepad with a number on it and a message that read,

[147]

"If you ever come to Texas, call me.
Love, Matthew."

I was a little hurt, but also relieved. He was a classy kid. And now I had a good reason to go to Texas. I showered and gathered myself and headed down to check out. The thought of riding the Harley back to California crossed my mind. It would give me time to think, time to air out the heat between Raoul and me. But it would seem that Mattie would not be the only thing missing in the morning. The Harley Neville had so lovingly bestowed upon me was gone. We'd parked it in the covered garage next to the D Hotel, but parked it was not when I returned.

"Shit," I cursed. Mattie couldn't have taken it. I still had the keys. So, what had happened? Where was the bike? After standing in the driveway for a moment, as the morning Vegas sun streamed in through the car garage, I decided to go back down to street level and take the Deuce back south to the PH. I called Neville to let him know the situation. To my chagrin he informed me of the situation, which in fact was the police had found his bikes and reported one in the fire pond at the Mirage and the other in the parking garage of the D Hotel and Casino. They'd both been retrieved. This was a bit of relief to me, and I was glad; it alleviated me of responsibility. He told me Raoul had spent the night in jail and was being charged with DWI, reckless driving and destruction of private property. He was still at the facility.

I hung up with Neville and walked the early morning streets where only tourists and bums gathered in the hopes of the new day. That was the point of it; after all, the American dream had changed from being self-made, to being made all of sudden by sheer luck, never minding the screw as you wasted your time with false messages of hope and fortune whether by lottery ticket or slot machine. And yet, even I placed my bets.

The sky was overcast, but the pink desert sun on the

horizon still shot through the muggy gray clouds, tempered though vibrant. Trash littered the ground, lifted and moved in the wind. Fremont Street was still alive, but even this was eerie in a dreamlike way against the ringing bells of slots and games, people asking you for a smoke, people who never went to bed. Same as me at the start of this trip. Over for now it would seem. I had accomplished what I had set out to do, which for the first time brought me great assurance. Even with Raoul temporarily incarcerated. My intentions now were only to jump the Deuce, get my things, and get home.

20

The general atmosphere of Neville's suite was stagnant and smoky. I pushed on the heavy door. It inched open gracefully. Light poured in from the vast window. The sky was a bold azure behind the looming Paris Hotel. I walked in, never minding the sleeping bodies littered against the walls and the back of the couch. It seemed not everyone left the party after all. I moved passed the tattered Bruce Willis costume, passed the view of the Eiffel Tower and the Bellagio Fountains and the Las Vegas Strip which was buzzing with life. The suite was quiet. The bar was a mess. Cigarette ash and butts dotted the floor.

I walked to the back of the suite where the master bedroom was. The door was closed. I opened it quietly as possible, in case Neville and Gladys were asleep. They were not. They were in a moment of coitus. Gladys straddled Neville and Neville's hands firmly clasped on each buttock, giving her lift as she bounced up and down on him.

"Oh," I accidentally exclaimed, actually stunned to walk in on my longtime friends in their most intimate of moments. Gladys immediately turned to the door shouting, "Oh, my god!" and fell over. Neville rolled over with her, the force of his weight projecting Gladys over the edge of the bed and exposing his wide, bare backside. I had turned away at that point, apologizing and closing the door. I walked back to the living room, and to the long red leather couch that sat elegantly before the panoramic windows. I hadn't seen him before, but there curled up in a fetal ball was Raoul. My heart dropped. His back was to the window and his arms were wrapped around himself. I hadn't seen him like that in years. I wondered at what point he had gotten out of jail. I would later find out that Neville wired his bail money and called him a cab. Even after fighting with him in the PH lobby and crashing his Harley into the volcano attraction at the Mirage. Neville had always had one of the biggest hearts I'd ever known.

I hesitated, unsure whether to wake him or let him be. I wasn't angry at him. In a way I had already forgiven him even if not verbally. Instances of the past rushed up on me. The type of timelines you've long forgotten. All the turmoil. A decade can make a lot of difference; so many actions taken; so many ways to change a person. But had I changed? Sometimes I felt I had remained radically the same. If not more amplified. I had become at peace with my past. I had shown love to that hurt child inside and reassured him that he was loved and that all would be well. I had nailed my heart open and learned compassion. Everything was a learning experience.

I sat next to Raoul by where he laid his head. He didn't use a pillow. I sat and looked down at him as he slept for a little bit as the light of the day shined in. The sky was a bold, deep blue with only wisps of clouds feathering the sky like thin, white veils. The past slowly started to fade away. He slept tenderly, a slight troubled look in his complexion, a visage of sadness. All parties end at some point or another. Still, I couldn't stand to see him like that. I caressed his hair, lightly rubbing his head, my fingers stroking his forehead and his cheek. Raoul began to stir. His eyes slowly opened and began to focus. He raised his hands up to his face as if to block the light and then looked up at me, consternation in his eyes. I gently grasped his jaw and lifted his face to look at mine, and, removing all the hurt and pity from my eyes, I smiled. Raoul

[151]

grabbed me and buried his face in my stomach, beginning to cry. He had taken me by surprise and I was almost too shocked to react. He wept, apologizing, refusing to unbury his face from my stomach. I eventually began to caress his head again. I lift him up, his docile frame against mine and embraced him. We stayed like that for a while on the couch and eventually laid down in spoons next to each other, not a word being said, simply the confidence of my spirit meshing with his and we drifted off as the buzz of Las Vegas Boulevard continued against the dancing fountains down below.

21

When behind the keyboard I am god. God, the generic creator. In the vast expanse of this continuum, the ultimate macrocosm, we micro-organisms fail to see, the majority anyway, what is beyond the explanation of the senses, science, religion, or politics, all the tenets of mental and emotional control, while experiencing in our carbon vessels. The idea seems to elude people. It is too big, I think. But there is also the paradox: nothing is certain, nothing is definite, no one is wrong and no one is right, because there is no way of knowing because we weren't there when it all began; at least, not that we recall. No one has a definite answer; which brings us to the point of death and what happens when you die. The fact of the matter is we are all made of energy at our most microscopic level; everything and anything is light waves and particles, so in essence everything is the same thing because it is made up of the same thing. And it all came from the same source energy that created everything in the known and unknown universes. If you never understood why hippie new-agers and the like tended to believe we are one, this is why. We, quite literally, are one. And each other's energy *does* affect the other. That's why when enough people understand an idea a lot of people seem to "get it" all at once.

There is an experiment with monkeys and other various

animals that test this theory. If you were lucky enough to be waking up in this time period, you would notice a lot of lights going off in the populace in general about the way the world is being run and what forces are actually holding the reigns of world history. It was beautiful to see, to know the power we held inside ourselves and know what we could do when we empowered ourselves.

I believed the hokey concept of becoming aware of everything upon death had much truth to it, and explained why the idea was perpetuated in our cultures. There would always be a complexity of just what life after death really was though for the most part I believed there was some type of life after death, unless, of course, you willed yourself into non-existence, or you returned to the Source from whence you came. Some people called that Nirvana. Because of these opposing views, I did believe that it was absolutely possible that what happened at the end of one's life could be determined by what that person believed in while living. And that that was the way of it for everyone. So if you believed there was heaven or hell, upon death, your conscious energy projected into some dimension of your own belief, heaven or hell, and from there the veil would slowly lift, you know, once you got passed your mental paradigm cage of what you thought existence was.

There was a particular hope in what we were doing though, because we believed by maintaining positive and higher energy that perhaps, for once, we could step into the light without first dancing with death. On this trip, this archetypical journey through the plunders of Sin City, I had flirted a few times with death. It had not been my first, and would most likely not be my last.

The road was always open and I'd already traveled much of it, by myself, with Raoul and even with Neville. There was only a matter of when and where, and the stories these travels brought. For the time being, the three of us would return to California. Raoul and I would make amends, and Gladys and Neville would exalt their excursion, taking with them all the memories created and embellishing the stories for weeks to come. Nevertheless, I had accomplished what I set out to do, which for the first time brought me great assurance. We were going to do it right, no matter what the cost, without resentment and without regrets. The lights of the Las Vegas Strip shrank in the distance.

—*Michael Aaron Casares*
Austin, TX
September 4, 2013

Michael Aaron Casares is a native Texan. He is the author of two volumes of poetry, This Reality of Man (2011, LT Press) and Sad Height (2005, Virgogray Press). He has also authored several chapbooks of poetry. He edits the online poetry journal, Carcinogenic Poetry, and serves as editor-in-chief of the literary culture magazine, Nothing. No One. Nowhere. He owns and operates Virgogray Press out of Austin, TX.